KT-220-626

MURDER AT THE FRINGE

First published in Great Britain in 1987 by
Polygon, 48 Pleasance, Edinburgh EH8 9TJ.

Copyright © Gordon DeMarco 1987.
All rights reserved.

Typeset by EUSPB, 48 Pleasance, Edinburgh EH8 9TJ.
Printed by Cox and Wyman, Reading, Berkshire.

Design by Tim Robertson
Illustration by Bill Reid

MURDER AT THE FRINGE

by

Gordon DeMarco

POLYGON
Edinburgh

CHAPTER ONE

I was sitting in the City Arts Centre Cafe staring into my second cappuccino. Old Jimmy, the newsboy, came through the door with a bundle of *The Scotsman* under his arm. I bought one, as I did most every morning. I wanted to play the stock market game on the business pages. One day I actually came within eighteen points of winning the daily thousand pound prize. Me and thirty thousand other suckers.

But I didn't get to the business section. There was a headline on page one that caught my eye instead. More like leaped out, grabbed me by the lapels and hollered in my face — *International Fringe Performer Murdered*.

The story underneath the headline said that Rodrigo Perez, the internationally famous Chilean Marxist play-wright was found dead up on Calton Hill last night. His skull had been crushed. According to a spokesman from his theatre company, Teatro Jara, Perez and his equally famous wife, actress Lily Montevideo, left the Assembly Rooms late last night following the last-minute, one-day postponement of the world première of Perez' contro-versial new play, *Ships in the Night*. It was thought they went for a late-night walk, but nobody could say for sure. The article said that the police were looking for Ms Montevideo, who had not returned to her hotel last night. The police were not offering any theories, but it sounded, from the article, like they were treating it as a murder-kidnapping.

I thought back to the little bit I knew about Rodrigo Perez. His plays, though broad, satiric comedies, had the reputation of going directly for the jugular of the enemy.

7

And the enemy was almost always the Latin American military officer corps, the multi-nationals or western imperialism in general. In *The General Came To Dinner*, it was Pinochet and the junta in Chile. And in *Once In Love With Henry*, it was the U.S. involvement in the coup that overthrew Allende in 1973.

Perez didn't spare the left from his pen, either. In *The Fairly Red Flag*, he savaged the old-line Stalinized communist parties, in Latin America as well as the Soviet union. Ecologists, anti-nuclear activists, Peronists, health food fadists, macho males and the save-the-whale crowd. They were fair game for Rodrigo Perez at one time or another.

Sometimes he appeared to stick one too many barbs into one too many sacred cows of the Latin American and international left. At least that's what some of those whose cows were stuck had claimed. Some truly disliked him politically and said so publicly, but that hardly seemed a motive for murder. On the whole, he was enthusiastically embraced by the left from theatre-going proletarians to Marxist culture vultures. The liberal middle classes adored him and several of his plays made it to the West End. If anyone had true cause to hate him it was the Latin American military juntas, the oil and beef barons and spooks for Western intelligence agencies. The papers said that the new play he had brought to the Fringe was a devastating exposé of the *Belgrano* affair.

So, maybe MI6, or some Whitehall Ministers, or perhaps some generals wearing sun-glasses, had cause to send Rodrigo Perez sailing off this mortal coil. But it sounded to me like he was simply the unfortunate victim of an old-fashioned American-style mugging that went wrong.

I finished my coffee and chatted briefly with Helen, the manager of the cafe, about the Festival. She told me some of the things she was planning to see. I took note.

8

It was eleven a.m. The day was still young and with nothing ahead of me but thirteen more hours, I decided to pootle over to the Assembly Rooms and book a show for the evening. Maybe even make a few casual enquiries about other things while I was at it.

I hiked up the Waverley Steps through the train station to Princes Street, the main drag in Edinburgh. From there I walked west to Frederick Street where I turned north. A block later I was on George Street where the Assembly Rooms, the premiere venue of the Fringe, is located.

But one doesn't simply "go" to the Assembly Rooms, however. One steps into the world of George Street, Edinburgh's answer to Manhattan's Madison Avenue in the upper sixties. It is lousy with wealth, upmarket shops and architectural grandeur. I always feel like I should wipe my feet and comb my hair before stepping onto one of its four blocks. Once I counted twenty-one banks and building societies and five life assurance companies between Charlotte and St. Andrew Squares. There are probably more. And there must be nearly as many fancy two-name shops. You know, the kind with just-so signs that announce you are entering the world of Highbrow and Stuffed Shirt furriers. Places like Lyon and Turnbull, Mappin and Webb, Hamilton and Inches. We have them in America, these two-name shops, although they're more likely to be called Croissants 'n Things.

The architecture of George Street, like most of Edinburgh, is real good on the eyes. I spent a year at Berkeley as an architecture student a long time ago so I know a thing or two. The street is like an outdoor museum with Glaswegian Edwardian baroques with splayed corners, Italian Renaissances, Corinthian pilastered frontages, doric porches and stately Georgian facades with sun-burst portals running all over the place. Funny, the things you remember from college.

The Assembly Rooms, by contrast, is a big, ugly building with one of those doric porches sitting on top of what looks like Romanesque arches in the middle of the block between Hanover Street and Frederick Street.

When I got there the joint was jumping. A magician who looked suspiciously like a middle-aged veteran from the Woodstock nation was doing a sleight of hand with some oranges and a grapefruit to a spellbound crowd of thirty. In the lobby I was met with a flood of leaflets on tables, floors, cigarette urns and in the hands of two mimes in white face and red nose passing them out to whoever would accept them. The fifty or so souls hanging around the box office, the information desk and to-ing and fro-ing from the cafe gave the place the look of Victoria Station at rush hour. I picked up a brochure from a table and headed for a vacant space along the wall to study the day's offerings.

Five minutes later I had narrowed my choice to one of the plays being performed by Hull Truck and a political cabaret featuring Mark Miwurdz, the socialist Mort Sahl from Sheffield. I settled for the cabaret.

I bought a ticket and then worked my way up the carpeted staircase, stepping over people eating filled rolls and poring over Fringe Guides. It looked like somebody had called a sit-in demonstration.

The place thinned out when I got to the bar, just down from the press office. In fact, it was the press bar. I ordered a lager and took it to a chair located around a small drinks table. On the other side of the table sat two men who looked a lot like they were working press. Only they weren't working. They were drinking. Both looked English. One was very large — okay, fat — and fifty. He looked like his lifelong hobby had been smoking cigarettes and guzzling Guinness. His face was red and puffy and he looked like a man who would always be out of breath. He had that look about him that said "gutter press". I guessed the *Sun*.

The other man was younger and healthier. Or, so he looked. In Britain, you can never be sure about things like that. He looked like the type who went to the right schools and drove the latest imported car. Probably lives in Chelsea and mixes his own muesli. I pegged him *Times* or *Telegraph*, but he could've been *Guardian*. Especially if he mixed his own muesli.

The two men were sitting next to each other staring vaguely in my direction. The fat man spoke out of the corner of his mouth to his colleague.

"What time is it?" he said.

The other man rolled his wrist and pushed back the sleeve of his coat. "It's nearly eleven-thirty," he said.

"Damn! That slag in the press office said there'd be a statement at eleven. I can't sit here all bleedin' day. I've got a one o'clock deadline."

"Does it really matter?"

"What?"

"Your deadline."

"Oh, leave off, will you? I don't need any stick from a wanking *Mail* theatre critic."

"You don't look like you need another drink either, Trev."

"Excuse me," I said leaning into their conversation. "I'm from the States. Covering the Festival for the, uh, San Francisco *Chronicle*."

The man from the *Mail* leaned forward and smiled. "A Yank! Waxlow here. The *Mail*." He extended his hand. I took it and gave it a shake. "This belligerent bugger," he said, pointing to his colleague who was trying to light a cigarette and paying only the remotest attention, "is Belker. He's with the *Times*. I must have looked surprised. "Surprised?" Waxlow said. I smiled. Waxlow smiled. Belker lit the wrong end of his cigarette.

"Belker," said Waxlow, trying to communicate with the man from the *Times*, who looked to be one short pint away from paralysis alcoholisis. "This chap is from the other side. America." Waxlow looked at me. "The San Francisco *Chronicle*, wasn't it?" I nodded.

"Bleedin' Yank!" spat Belker, looking at a man sitting at the next table.

Waxlow smiled nervously. "I'd apologize for him if I thought it'd do any good," he said. "But I'm afraid he's like that when he's sober, too."

"No apologies necessary," I said.

"San Francisco *Chronicle*?" Belker burped. I don't know, maybe he has small pores that slows down messages getting to the brain. "You from San Francisco?" he asked, putting one and one together.

"That's right," I said.

"You one of them bleedin' poofs?"

Waxlow turned to Belker and rolled his eyes. "Belker, why don't you just pass out and be done with it."

"I'm not pissed. That's what you think, innit? That I'm pissed. Well, sod you! I am not pissed. Just a little happy, that's all."

"If you get any happier, old man, you'll land us all in the nick for creating a public disturbance."

"Bollocks!"

Waxlow shrugged his shoulders and turned to me. "He opened the place this morning. My guess is that he's been knocking back the lager since the night train left from King's Cross. We're both here waiting for a statement from the press office concerning last night's murder of Rodrigo Perez. You did hear about it?"

"I did. That's what I wanted to ask you boys about."

"He i'nt a poof, is he, Waxlow?" asked Belker, staring past both of us. "Don't fancy bein' around bleedin' poofs. They can give you A.I.D.S."

"For God's sake, man, will you be still?" said Waxlow, raising his voice a noticeable octave.

"As long as he i'nt no bleedin' poof. That's all I ask."

"And he's one of the best they have at the *Times*," said Waxlow tilting his head toward his lager-soaked colleague. "The *Sun*'s been trying to get him for years." He looked at Belker. "But the man does have his principles." Both Waxlow and I laughed.

"I read that Lily Montevideo disappeared," I said, trying to get back to the subject.

Waxlow knitted his brows. "Well, she's missing. I think there's a difference there."

"I think the cow bashed in her boyfriend's brains," said Belker, not sounding half as stewed as he had a moment before, "and then sloped off to parts unknown."

Waxlow turned in his chair to Belker. "I didn't think you were still with us, Trev," he said.

"Shows what you know, dunnit?"

"Well, what evidence do you have to substantiate that remarkable theory?"

"I don't need no bleedin' evidence. I've seen this kind of thing a hundred times before. It's bloody human nature, that's what it is. I know."

Waxlow looked at me. "The poor bastard's been writing the same story for so long he's starting to believe it himself. Bad sign, that. But that's what the *Times* wants. The *Mail*, too. So, that's what we give them."

Before we had a chance to launch into a discussion on the larger issues of British journalism, we heard a loud commotion coming from the direction of the press office. A dozen men and women scurried from the press bar and up the steps where the Assembly Rooms press office is located.

"That's it!" shouted Belker, jumping from his chair.

"The long-awaited press statement," Waxlow added informatively as he rose to his feet. "Come along,

13

old man. You don't want to miss this one." I followed Waxlow out of the bar and we both followed Belker who was bulldozing his way through a covey of reporters trying to jam into one of the small interview rooms next to the press office.

After a moment of polite shoving, Belker excepted, quiet obtained. I was just outside the open doorway standing nose-to-ear with a man who looked to be enjoying it. The steady, business-like voice of a woman I couldn't see began reading the press statement:

"Last night, Mr. Rodrigo Perez, author and director of *Ships in the Night*, a new play that was scheduled for premiere at the Assembly Rooms, was found dead on Calton Hill. Ms Lily Montevideo, star of *Ships in the Night* and wife to Mr. Perez, who is believed by the authorities to have been with Mr. Perez last night, is as of ten o'clock this morning listed as a missing person by the police. The Assembly Rooms regrets to announce that it has been forced to once again postpone the opening of *Ships in the Night*. If and when it is rescheduled a statement will be issued from this office. Thank you."

The moment the press officer stopped speaking the room erupted with a din that could only be compared to Question Time in the House of Commons. Men and women began shouting questions at the top of their lungs.

"Was Miss Montevideo kidnapped?"

"Was there any sign of a struggle?"

"Who do the Perez people think killed him?"

"Where is Pete Swallow?"

"Has there been a statement from the Chilean government?"

"How much money does the Assembly Rooms stand to lose with the cancellation of the play?"

"Is there a love triangle element involved.?"

And those were only the easy questions. The press

officer announced that she was in no position to answer any of the questions and walked out of the room amid a chorus of protests and more questions.

The room became unpacked almost as quickly as it had become packed. Belker was nearly trotting as he came past where Waxlow and I were standing. Waxlow held out his arm and hooked the lumbering Belker.

"Hey, Trev. What's the hurry?" he said.

Belker stopped and gave Waxlow a sarcastic glance. "Deadline, mate. Some of us got to work for a living." Belker seemed a changed man. A sober man.

"I'm almost afraid to ask," said Waxlow. "What is your story?"

"Like I said. The slag topped him and scrammed with the leading man. Or something like that."

"I should've known." Waxlow turned to me. "Remember, you read it first in the *Times*."

"I'd really like to stay here and chat with you ladies," Belker said with a grin he didn't mean, "but I've got . . ."

"Yes, we know," said Waxlow holding up his hand. "A deadline."

"Right." Belker backed away. "See you when I see you."

"Cheerio."

Belker hitched up his pants, turned and scrambled away in the direction of the stairs.

"People like Trev," said Waxlow, almost wistfully, "make the newspaper game what it is today." Waxlow then excused himself. He said he was reviewing Hull Truck who were performing in the Music Hall in twenty minutes.

"God, I hope they have some fresh material this year," he said, rolling his eyes toward the ceiling. He shook my hand and disappeared down the staircase into the Assembly Rooms traffic.

CHAPTER TWO

It wasn't even noon. I had more than seven hours to kill before the political cabaret. I took out my Fringe Guide and started thumbing through its ninety pages looking for an afternoon's diversion. One-person shows on the lives of Harold Macmillan, Stan Laurel, Gracie Fields, McGonnigal and three different Oscar Wildes. These were squared off against cabaret reviews with such improbable names as The Dead Reagans, Fru Fru Kerfuffle and the Cockups, and A Fizz Punch Flip Zombie Sidecar Pick-me-up. And that's not mentioning the Malvinas Cabaret.

And these were in competition with two productions of Hamlet — one from Aberdeen University and the other an all-woman cast from the Hackney Wimmins Theatre Project — a Steven Berkoff play, and a production of Brecht's *Good Woman of Szchuan* from a company in Manchester. And that was only the first twenty pages.

I decided instead to nip over to my aunt's place in Leith for some lunch. Aunt Gina was the reason I came to Edinburgh in the first place. I mean a good Italian-American boy from San Francisco away from the mother country for the first time must pay his respects to his grandfather's youngest sister, right? The original plan was to stop over in London for a week or so, take in a couple shows and then go up to Edinburgh for a weekend with the relatives before heading to the Mediterranean — France, Italy, Greece — where I intended to do some serious laying about on those white sandy beaches the travel brochures rave about.

Well, since that weekend with Aunt Gina and Uncle Tony, the closest I've gotten to the Mediterranean was a few months ago when I went down to The Oval in Brixton for a cricket match.

No, Edinburgh's physical beauty and Aunt Gina's

cooking made the city on the Forth an ideal place to sit out 1984. Away from the political primaries, the conventions, the Olympics, the election, newspeak and doublethink. Not to mention my former life in San Francisco. It all seems like it was such a long time ago.

Although I come from an Italian family, I'm second generation American. My grandfather was a fisherman from the old country who settled in the North Beach section of San Francisco along with thousands of other Italian immigrants. He and my grandmother moved to the Sunset district when they got a few dollars ahead. My father and mother moved to Daily City, just south of town, before I was born. And by the time I graduated high school we were living in South San Francisco. So, during my early years, my links with the old Italian community in North Beach were practically non-existent.

So, that was another reason to visit Aunt Gina and Uncle Tony. I wanted to get back to my roots. However, if anyone had told me I'd find them in Scotland I would have laughed in their face. But Scotland it was to be. In Leith, the old Italian neighbourhood. My father had ceased being Italian when his father moved the family out of North Beach and he always made fun of his relatives in Edinburgh. "A bunch of spaghetti-benders in kilts," he used to say about Gina and Tony. He wasn't malicious about it, but he had that unmistakable air of someone who has been de-ethnicized and is proud of it. He even changed the family name from Conigliaro to Connors. Until I got to high school, I thought we were of English stock. Papa wasn't too happy when I changed my name back. And he hates to be called "Papa". "Call me Dad, godamnit!" he always says to me. He sort of looks down his nose at me the way he did at Gina and Tony because they aspired to nothing more than having a little restaurant of their own.

17

Wee Fiore is on Leith Walk about halfway between the Playhouse, which is just below Calton Hill, and the Kirkgate down near the docks. It was more a cafe than a real Italian restaurant. That is, upon request, you could be served chips with nearly everything on the menu. And of course that's just what the British like to do. But Aunt Gina makes a minestrone that starts violins playing in the Via Veneto. And there are other things, too, that make Wee Fiore different from the traditional peas-and-gravy British caff. A large poster of Naples is one of the differences. Both Gina and Tony come from the area near there. A place called Frosinone. A place I was on my way to visit about two years ago.

The cafe wasn't too busy. The lunchtime crowd was still a half-hour away. The smell of minestrone and parmesan greeted me as I walked through the door. So did Aunt Gina.

"Rocco!" she said, nearly shouting, as she scurried from behind the counter and threw her arms around me. "I thought sure you died. You don't come to visit your Aunt Gina anymore."

"Sorry, Aunt Gina," I said, returning her embrace. "Just been busy lately, I guess."

"Busy? Busy with your lassie, that's what I think." She walked behind the counter and looked toward the kitchen door. "Hey, Tony!" she shouted. "Come, look who's here. Back from the dead."

Uncle Tony came through the kitchen door wiping his hands on the skirt-length apron he had tied about his waist. "Rocco!" he said. He took my hand and shook it like it was a knife and he was slicing prosciutto. He looked at Aunt Gina. "See, Gina, I told you he was still in Edinburgh. Gina says to me, Tony, she says, that boy's gone back to California."

I smiled. "Still here," I said.

"And still hungry, I bet," said Aunt Gina, taking my

elbow in her hand. "Come, you sit down. The minestrone's just made. I'll get you a nice big bowl."

"You're a doll, Aunt Gina," I said, taking a seat at the counter.

"Ach, aye, I'm a doll when you're hungry. You're just like your grandfather. What do you hear from home, Rocco?"

"Gina!" Uncle Tony scolded. "First, the soup."

"Ach, aye. Plenty of time for my bletherin' after you've had something to eat." She turned and went to the stove and stirred the large pot that contained the minestrone.

"Rocco," said Uncle Tony, "I've got to get back to the kitchen just now and get the chips started or I'll lose half my customers. You come over to the house tonight for your tea, okay?"

"I can't tonight, Uncle Tony. But soon. I promise."

Tony pointed a finger at me and smiled. "I hold you to your promise. Ciao, Rocco."

"Ciao, Uncle Tony."

As he disappeared into the kitchen, Aunt Gina brought me a large bowl of steaming hot minestrone, a half a loaf of Italian bread and a bottle of chianti. She placed the food in front of me and uncorked the wine and filled my glass. "You eat and we talk," she said.

"Sure," I replied, slurping the first savoury spoonful of soup.

"You had us worried, Rocco. I almost called your papa, but Tony talked me out of it. I thought maybe you started doing what you used to do in America and got into some trouble."

"Investigation work? Naw, not me. That's one of the main reasons I left San Francisco. To get away from all that."

"Well, that is very good to hear Rocco. I was afraid to pick up the paper in the morning. I thought maybe you got mixed up in some nasty business or something. Leith has turned into such a bad place the last few years. Drugs, stabbings, robberies. Ach, not at all like the old days when a person felt safe to walk the streets of their own neighbourhood. I'm afraid to leave the house at night now. He won't say so, but your Uncle Tony is afraid too. Promise me you don't do investigations into dangerous things like that."

I held up my right hand. "I promise."

"On the head of your mother and father and ten saints of your choice."

I laughed and promised to keep my nose clean.

"That's a good boy," she said. "You finish your soup. There's plenty more. I've got to check on Tony. See if we've got enough chips for the dinner crowd." She turned and disappeared through the kitchen door.

I reached over and picked up the copy of *The Scotsman* lying at the end of the counter and reread the story about the Perez murder. What was he doing on Calton Hill at midnight I wondered?

Aunt Gina reappeared through the kitchen door. "Eat some more soup, Rocco," she said, reaching for my bowl.

"I've still got plenty," I protested.

"I'll get some more bread." She turned away to slice a baguette.

"Aunt Gina," I said, as she placed a fresh plate of bread in front of me. "What would you think of a person who took a midnight stroll on Calton Hill?"

"I'd say he was barmy," she replied matter-of-factly.

"Why is that?"

"It's a very nasty place, that's why. Ask your cousin Rudy. He used to be mixed up with all that nasty business when he was younger. If it hadn't been for some of his mates at Bilston our Rudy might've turned to a life of crime. I hate to say such a thing about my own son,

20

but he came that close." She held up her thumb and forefinger about an inch apart.

"What goes on up there?"

She brushed her hand across her chest. "What do I know? Ask Rudy. He'll tell you. What do you want to know about such a place, Rocco? Is it about that murder in the paper? You're not mixed up with that, are you, son? You promised me you weren't mixed up with such things."

"I'm not. Just curious, that's all. You think Rudy will drop by here after work?"

"Who knows what Rudy will do? He comes to see me about as often as you do."

"I promise I'll come by for a meal, okay?"

"Tonight?"

"Not tonight, but soon, Aunt Gina. I promise."

"That's just what Rudy says. 'Soon.' Uh-oh, here comes my dinner customers." I turned to see two groups of middle-aged people, mostly women, push open the door and enter. "I've got to go now, Rocco. You come by the house 'soon', okay?"

"This weekend. I'll call you."

"You be a good boy, Rocco."

"Thanks for the soup, Aunt Gina. If you see Rudy, tell him I was asking for him. Tell him to phone me."

"And you do the same. You'll probably see him before his mother does."

CHAPTER THREE

It was the kind of day that had one of those glorious British skies. The kind that people in Montana like to brag about. Mediterranean blue with fat cumulus clouds waddling across the ionisphere. The kind of sky

21

Constable might have painted if he'd had some brighter colours in his paint-box. Ever since I saw a movie called "The Draughtsman's Contract", a thirty-five millimetre feast of language, politics and rural colour, I've called such spectacles "Draughtsman's sky".

The sky pulled me up Leith Walk toward Calton Hill. It was subconscious propulsion to get to a place that provided a view. Also, it was the scene of the crime and there was nothing subconscious about that.

Calton Hill is located beyond the east end of Princes Street and is one of the smallest of Edinburgh's seven hills. But it is one of the most interesting. It is a repository for monuments and public buildings. Some might say a dumping ground. There's Nelson's Monument, a hundred-foot tower that looks more like a nineteenth-century nautical spyglass. Then the old Royal Observatory and monuments to William Playfair, the architect of much of Georgian Edinburgh, and someone called Dugald Stewart. Then the curious row of columns they call the National Monument: just seven Greek columns standing as the porch to a building that was never built.

I climbed the steps from Waterloo Place onto the gravel road that winds around the north face of the hill. From there the hill looks out over Leith and Portobello. I stopped. The huge blue cranes of the port stood motionless. I thought it might have been a lunchtime break, but as I scanned the docks I learned the real reason for the inactivity. There were no ships! At least none that I could see. Not even an old tub or two in drydock. Further proof that post-industrial Britain was living up to its name.

Many of the smokestacks in Leith appeared to be idle as well. Except for one that was releasing a small, dense, ochre-coloured pollutant. It hung lazily above the smokestack looking for someplace to go.

The Forth looked a lot less menacing. A lot like the

San Francisco Bay. In fact, Calton Hill reminds me of a larger version of Telegraph Hill. Calton Hill is much greener than California hillsides in August, but the view is similar.

I walked around the hill to the National Monument. It looked like a good place for muggers to convene and plan out a night of mayhem. Lots of good places to lurk. I tried to remember if the article in *The Scotsman* identified the spot where Perez was found. I don't believe it did. That seemed strange since it is such a big place and there are numerous distinct parts to it. There is even a paved road that empties into a car-park between the National Monument and the Observatory. The killer or killers didn't have to be on foot. They could have driven up and driven away. Might explain how Lily Montevideo was kidnapped.

I continued around the hill. The washing on the line in the garden at the base of Nelson's Monument flapped energetically in the breeze. The sounds of a radio programme coming from the monument-keeper's quarters rode itinerant gusts of wind in several directions.

A number of people were sitting in their vehicles in the car-park, reading newspapers and smoking cigarettes. Tourists with cameras were taking pictures of the Scott Monument and the castle. And there was a woman holding an empty lead calling for a mutt named "Rufus". Everything was as it should have been. Ordinary as beer and filled rolls.

If I was looking for clues I didn't find any. But then, who said I was looking? I left Frisco, in part, to get away from all that. Seven years as a private investigator. Most of the time it was lousy. Following husbands and wives who weren't married to each other; looking under workers fingernails to make sure they weren't smuggling machine tools out of their factories; bugging phones in the financial district; skip-tracing. Lousy stuff. I got mixed up in the business in the first place because I believed what guys like Chandler and Hammett wrote. I expected every job to be a 'caper', every crook to be a 'gunsel' and all the women to look like Mary Astor or Lauren Bacall. Okay, so I was stupid. But a college dropout with limited resources didn't have a whole lot of choices in the seventies. At least this college dropout with limited resources didn't.

But I must say the last two years of it weren't half bad. Generally speaking. I did a lot of freelance work for lawyers. Not the kind who chase ambulances, but those who chase causes. Good causes. I tracked down witnesses and researched cases against corporate polluters and the like.

But it all caught up with me one day when I tracked down a reluctant witness and brought her back to town to testify against one of those corporate polluters with mob connections. She was gunned down on Bryant Street while I was holding her arm and reassuring her that everything was going to be alright. That was it for me. I took it as a sign. God's way of telling me to get out of town by sundown. I didn't quite make it by sundown, but I did make it and that was the important thing.

Since that time the closest I've gotten to detective work has been tracking down "The Rockford Files" on BBC2. For some reason the Beeb keeps changing the day and time. Keeps me on my toes, though.

CHAPTER FOUR

Morag is an actress who owns the flat just off Broughton Street that I've called home for the last year. It's a small place, but she's away in London most of the time looking for work. When she's in Edinburgh she stays in the little bedroom off the kitchen. I've got the big one. It's a good arrangement, having the whole place to myself most of the time and only paying half the rent. When she's in town the flat gets crowded, but we manage to stay out of each other's hair.

Morag had been in Edinburgh for the past two weeks preparing for her one-woman show in the Fringe Festival. She was doing the life of Emma Goldman, the American revolutionary anarchist. She had opened the night before. I would've gone, but she made me promise to wait a few days until all the kinks got worked out.

She was sitting at the kitchen table smoking a cigarette and staring blankly at the poster of fresh herbs that hung on one of the walls. Lillian, her cat, lay curled up in her lap. I said hello, but Morag took no notice.

"Tea?" I said, walking over to the drainboard next to the sink where the electric kettle was plugged into the wall.

Morag turned around with a fright. "What? Oh. Oh, it's you, Rocco. I guess I didn't hear you come in."

"I could've marched in with half the pipers from the Tattoo and I don't think you would've heard that, either. Thinking about last night's show?"

"I suppose." She looked at me, but her eyes were unfocused."

"What happened, for God's sake? Did you lay an egg or what?"

"Lay an egg?"

"Bomb. Slip on a banana peel. Flop. Take a dive into the toilet."

"No, nothing like that. In fact, it went a little better than I expected."

"Well, what, then?" The kettle started bubbling. I turned it off. "You look like the vet has just told you Lillian has cancer of the whiskers and only has six weeks to live."

Morag didn't say anything right away. She was looking at the poster on the wall like she was studying for an O-Level on marjoram and sweet basil. She turned to me. "What? What did you say about Lillian?"

"Skip it. You want regular or herbal?"

"Tea?"

"No, cocaine. Say, what's got into you, Morag? Your head's somewhere in the Highlands."

"Did you hear about Rodrigo Perez?"

"Yeah. Nasty business, that."

"It's so unreal. I knew him."

"You did?" I put teabags into two cups and carried them to the table. I put one of the cups in front of Morag and slid into the chair at the opposite end of the table. I got a good look at her face for the first time. Her eyes were red and her cheeks damp.

"I worked with him before. The last time was at the Royal Court about two years ago. It's such a shock. And they say Lily's been kidnapped. Who would do such a thing?"

"You tell me. Who had it in for Perez enough to murder him? The Chilean secret police?"

"I don't know, Rocco. I haven't seen Rodrigo or Lily since the Royal Court. I know they were both very security conscious. I remember Rodrigo telling me that he had trouble with rowdies before. He was beaten up once. It was a political thing. Other than that, I know bugger all. It's such a bloody shock. You know, I was supposed to meet with him this morning."

"Oh, really?"

"Aye. He called me a couple of days ago from London and said he wanted us to get together. I mean I worked with the man, but we weren't that close personally. Oh, not that he didn't try, but I never let my personal life get mixed up with my work. Not even when it's Rodrigo Perez."

26

"Was there anybody who was close to him? Any friends, actors, that sort of thing?"

"I don't know. Two years ago it would have been Pete Swallow."

"Who is Pete Swallow?"

"He is Teatro Jara's business manager. Arranges bookings, tours, runs the school and keeps the books. Things like that. A big wanker if you ask me."

"How's that?"

"He's so bloody English. So City of London business-like all the time. He took himself very seriously and treated the actors in the company like shite. A real arrogant bastard."

"Arrogant enough to kill the head man?"

Morag laughed cynically. "Hardly. He's a bully, but only to those he thinks are below him. He worshipped the ground Rodrigo and Lily walked on."

"More tea?" I asked. Morag shook her head. "How about a biscuit?" I added, trying to ease the conversation away from the Perez murder. Again she shook her head. "I've got a packet of McVitie's chocolate-covered digestives," I coaxed. "Milk chocolate." Morag didn't even bother to shake her head. She was staring into her teacup.

"Say," I said, reaching across the table and placing my hand on top of hers. "Tell me more about the play. How did it go last night?"

"Do you really think the Chilean police had anything to do with it?" Morag looked straight into my face for the first time since I sat down.

"With what? Your play?" I laughed alone.

"Who could have killed Rodrigo?"

"Maybe it was just a mugging that went bad. My aunt says Calton Hill is a nasty place when the sun goes down."

"Don't be silly. We both ken it was nothing like

27

that. Muggers don't kill and kidnap people. This isn't America. This is wee Scotland we're talking about."

"Yeah, you're right. But there's nothing we can do about it."

Morag's eyes came to life. She took a sip of cold tea and leaned forward in her chair. "I remember you telling me when you first moved in that you were some kind of investigator back in America."

"Used to be, luv. About a hundred-and-twenty-five years ago."

"It's clear the police will do bugger all to find who killed poor Rodrigo and kidnapped Lily. We'll need someone with your skills to find the murderers. You could do it, you know, Rocco. We would pay you, too."

"Hold on just a minute." I got up from my chair and went to the sink and poured out the half-inch of tea that remained in my cup, rinsing it out. I placed the cup in the drain rack and turned to Morag. "I said I used to do investigation work. That's as in 'not doing it anymore'. I'm retired. Washed up. Besides, I never worked on a murder case. I wouldn't know the first thing to do. And who's this 'we', anyway?"

"Actors. Rodrigo was an inspiration to the theatre in this country. In the world. You don't have to be a Marxist to appreciate his work. He was a genius who spoke to all kinds of people. He was our Bertolt Brecht. He was more than that. He was . . ."

Morag's eyes began filling up with tears. She turned her head away from me and began weeping silently. I pulled a McVitie's from the packet and popped it into my mouth in two bites. I looked out the kitchen window at a woman stringing her washing from two poles in the courtyard below. I wanted to go out there and talk with her. Anything to get out of the flat and leave Morag to her grief. Not that I was unsympathetic, but because I believe it is something that is done best alone. I couldn't, however, find the courage to leave.

I polished off another biscuit and walked over to Morag. Lillian jumped off her lap and scampered out of the kitchen. I put a reassuring hand on Morag's shoulder. I could feel her body quaking.

"If it'll make you feel any better," I said, "I could ask a few questions and maybe nose around a bit."

Morag's head snapped around. "Oh, aye," she said, smiling. "That would be lovely. It would mean so much to know that you're working on the case." Morag's tears had dried and her eyes were focused and in charge of the situation. Quite a transformation, that. I was looking forward to seeing her Emma Goldman performance more than ever.

CHAPTER FIVE

So, what's a few questions? That's not really getting involved. It's doing a friend a favour, that's all. That's what I told myself all the way to the pub at the top of Leith Walk. Rudy stopped in there sometimes on his way home from work. It was almost 3 p.m. The morning shift at Bilston Glen would be over. I figured if he was still stopping at the pub he'd be by within the next thirty minutes.

I ordered a half pint of heavy and took a table where I could keep an eye on the door. The pub was pretty quiet. I used to go there a lot mainly for that reason. Basically a workers' boozer. Most of them like Rudy, miners. It was a good place to go if you wanted to keep current with the class struggle.

Except for a couple of geezers standing at the far end of the bar, the place was deserted. I was half-way through my drink when one of the voices at the bar broke the dull silence like a glass ashtray falling to a marble floor.

"Ya bloody Trotskyite bastard!" it bellowed. "They should shoot the whole bloody lot of yous." The man with the voice turned and began stomping away. Before he reached the door our eyes met. It was Jocky Brown. He stopped and pointed a wobbly finger at me. "And there's another bloody one!"

"Jocky," I said with a broad smile, "what are you drinking?"

"I'll no' be taking a drink wi' the likes of you."

"Still drinking lager and whisky?"

"Just plain lager. The doctor told me to leave the whisky alone for a while. The bloody bastard."

"Another Trotskyite, no doubt."

"Aye. It widny surprise me."

"Well, don't just stand there. Come on and sit down while I get you a drink."

Jocky moved without another word and sat down at my table. I got up to go to the bar for his drink.

"Since yer buyin', lad," he said, "I'm changin' my order."

"Oh?"

"Aye. Ya can git me a Scunthorpe Sunrise."

"What in the world is that?"

"Ya dinna want ta ken."

"You're right."

"Ya might get us a bag of nuts while you're at it, lad," he said.

Jocky Brown was a retired miner. Probably pushing seventy, he was lean and hard with a ruddy red face, topped with thick, wavy white hair that made him look a little like a strawberry sundae. He was a friend of Rudy's and would often sit with us when Rudy and I were in the pub.

Jocky had been with the Communist Party almost since it was formed. He loved talking about World War II and Stalin. He knew a lot about both. He had been a sergeant in a Scottish regiment that was involved in the capture of Berlin. A Russian soldier traded hats with him and Jocky still had it. Sometimes he even wore it, especially when he anticipated a fight with the Trotskyists, Eurocoms or anyone else who took exception to his fervently held Stalinist convictions. The Soviet Union was to him what the New Testament is to a born-again Christian or the Age of Aquarius was to a hippie.

Jocky also had another, more reasonable passion. Robert Burns and Scottish literature. This made him more tolerable and in his own cantankerous way, even likeable. In January he had invited Rudy and me to be his guests at his club's annual Burns Supper. And that was an experience for me. From the piping in of the haggis and the club president's recitation of Burns' ode to same, to the traditional supper of haggis, tatties and neeps, the endless rounds of drinking, singing Burns' songs and energetic dramatizations of some of his poems. At the end Jocky treated everyone in the hall to a spirited, melodramatic rendering of "Tam o' Shanter". This was the Jocky I liked. However, it was the other Jocky, the Stalinist zealot, the "tankie", as these birds are sometimes called, that was waiting for me when I returned with his drink and nuts.

"Have you seen Rudy in here, lately," I said, trying to take command of the conversation.

"Ach! And he's another one, too," Jocky said derisively a split second before taking a generous swallow of lager.

"Why don't we forget World War II for a little bit. What do you say?"

"You'd bloody well like that, wouldn't you. You'd like to forget that the Soviet Union saved your bacon. Yes, you'd rather talk about counter-revolution. Poland, maybe, and your bloody pope."

"He's not *my* bloody pope. I'd rather talk about Rodrigo Perez."

"Who?"

"Rodrigo Perez. You know, the Marxist playwright who was murdered last night."

"Marxist playwright! Anti-Marxist playwright, you mean. I've read about his plays. Anti-party bastard. Got what he bloody well deserved if you ask me."

"Meaning just what?"

"Meaning all the anti-communist rubbish he's been writing all these years maybe finally caught up with him. Maybe he was given an old-fashioned dose of proletarian justice."

"Having a person's head bashed in by thugs in the dead of night is proletarian justice?"

"I widny be so quick ta believe what the capitalist press says, lad. Just a lot of wankin' if ya want ta ken the truth. I dinnae ken who topped your pal. Maybe he was an MI6 agent and had a falling out with his bosses and they took care a' him. Or maybe it was the CIA. Sounds like something those bloody bastards would do. But whoever it was did a big favour to the international working class movement. Ya can believe me that."

"Sure. The biggest favour since martial law in Poland. That was a giant step for socialism."

Jocky's eyes grew as large as two "Coal Not Dole" badges. His red face became even redder and his breathing sounded laboured, like he had just done a couple of laps around Arthur's Seat. He balled his hand into a fist and shook it at me like he meant it. "Yer no' still a Solidarity man, are ya?" It was an accusation, not a question.

"Yes, I am," I said. "I'd like to see socialism given a chance."

"You mean the fascist Catholic Church given a chance. They're behind that whole business. Them and your CIA." Jocky took a large gulp of his lager. Then he put his glass down on the table, leaned forward and looked straight into my eyes. "Do ya no' believe in the class struggle, son?" he said, with the frightening sincerity of a priest asking a parishioner if he believed in the virgin birth.

"I don't believe in terrorizing the working class of Poland and murdering radical playwrights."

"Ya daft bugger. Ya sound more like a bloody Trotskyite everytime I see you."

"And you, Jocky, sound . . ." Before I could think of something to say, I saw Rudy walk into the pub. I waved my hand, hailing him over to my table.

"Rocco," he said. "What are you doing with this old tankie blowhard?"

"Who ya calling a blowhard?" Jocky said somewhat belligerently.

Rudy ignored him. "What are you and this old punter drinking?"

"I'm drinking heavy and Jocky is back to straight lager."

"I'll no' stop ya from buyin' me a pint," Jocky said, "but don't expect me to sit here and drink it with the likes of you. I ken when I'm outnumbered by the class enemy."

Rudy shook his head and walked away toward the bar. Jocky and I sat in silence until Rudy returned with the drinks. Jocky took his and excused himself.

"I like you lads, right enough," he said in parting, "but no' when ya talk your political rubbish. It gets right up ma nose." He raised his glass towards us and walked away. Over to two men standing at the bar. The ones he had stomped away from minutes before. I wondered if they believed in the class struggle.

CHAPTER SIX

Although he looked much older, Rudy was only in his early thirties. He was taller than most Scots. Darker, too, as were most Italo-Scots in Edinburgh. There's something about people from the northern climates. You can spot them right away. The lack of sun and a mountain of potatoes, the average yearly consumption in Britain, do something to the complexion.

Rudy would never be accused of being a native, although he was. On his lean, dark face sat a Zapata moustache like a limp horseshoe. His face was already lined and cracked, grown that way during the years working underground at Bilston Glen.

The look he wore on that face was hard to describe. Like maybe he had a chip on his shoulder or something. Ready for a punch-up if the right situation presented itself. Maybe it was a relic of the days when he was a punk and ran with a gang. More likely, it was a souvenir of the miners' strike.

"Rocco, what brings you to the Shit and Shovel?" Rudy asked with a smile, staring at Jocky pad across the pub floor. "I haven't seen you for months."

"Well, cousin, I've come with a message from the boss."

"Mama?"

"The same. She said if I see that no good Rudy to tell him to come visit his mother and father and that I should give you their address in case you forgot where they live."

Rudy laughed. "Aye. I've been meaning to call. I have,

34

really. But they've been giving us a lot of stick at Bilston lately. We've had meetings almost every day to deal with harassment from management. It's getting bloody awful. Worse than before the strike. In fact, we've got another meeting tonight. Management sacked a bloke for slagging off one of the scabs. He's the third one they've sacked this month."

"Hey! You don't have to explain anything to me. I'm just a messenger."

"Ken. I'll give her a call tonight, okay?"

"She's your mother. You know best."

"So, she sent you here to give me the business, eh?"

It was my turn to laugh. "No, not really. I stopped by the cafe today for lunch. She read the riot act to me as well."

"She has a way of making a bloke feel guilty without even trying."

"Yes. It's a gift."

"So, then. Two guilty blokes getting pissed in the Shit and Shovel. How are you, Rocco? What've you been up to?"

"Funny you should ask. I was sitting in the City Art Centre Cafe this morning reading about the murder up on Calton Hill last night."

"Rodrigo Perez?"

"Yeah. You know about him?"

"Some. I went to London a few years back with a couple of mates. We saw *The Fairly Red Flag*."

"Yeah, well, now he's dead."

"Ken. Hey, you're not working on the case or anything, are you? I thought you'd given up all that cops and robbers bit."

"Just curious, that's all. Like about what goes on up on Calton Hill at night that could get someone topped. Aunt Gina said I should ask you. She said you used to be a regular little capo in the Midlothian underworld."

"She did, did she? How do you like that?"

"A mother's love works in strange and mysterious ways."

"She must be dead sore at me. I really will give her a call. Tomorrow at the latest. I promise."

"Rudy. Whether or not you call your mother is your business. Personally, I think you'd be a big knucklehead if you put it off much past that, but who am I to say? What's really on my mind at the moment is Calton Hill night-life. I don't want you telling any tales out of school, but I know you used to run with some pretty tough customers. Come on, tell me. What goes on up there after the sun goes down?"

"It was a long time ago, Rocco. Ancient history."

"My major in college."

"What?"

"Skip it. You were saying."

"It used to be a place to pinch a few purses. Sniff some glue. Things like that."

"That all? Hell, they do that in the doorways of most of the housing estates in this town."

"Well, that's all I did."

"Okay, Rudy. If it'll help, I'll grant you immunity from prosecution."

"What?"

"Hey, look, I don't want a confession. Just an idea of the scene up there."

"Well, I hear that it's turned into a place poofs go for a good time."

"Perez wasn't gay, as far as I know."

"I've also heard that it's turned into a pretty heavy drug scene."

"Heavier than when you were there?"

"Much heavier. Hard drugs. Like bought and sold. Lots of money changing hands."

"Hard drugs?"

"Heroin and cocaine. They hard enough? One of my mates from the old days tells me the stuff comes right into the port from Asia and South America. On legitimate cargo ships and passenger liners. Calton Hill is one of the places they take the stuff and wholesale it to the street pushers."

"Now, that's interesting. Do you know if any ships docked down at Leith that might be carrying?"

"Rocco. It's all pub talk. One geezer tells another. A third tells my mate and he tells me. It's no' exactly reliable information, you know."

"Got the names of any ships?"

"You are working on a case aren't you?"

"I promised a friend I'd ask a few questions, that's all."

"Well, I heard there was a small passenger ship down at the Albert Dock. It's from South America. It might be carrying a shipment of heroin. I don't know. I heard it off a bloke in a club."

"Rudy, let me buy you a drink."

CHAPTER SEVEN

After I left Rudy at the pub I thought I'd mosey down to the docks. Seemed like the logical place to go. I still had almost three hours to kill before Mark Miwurdz and the political cabaret was scheduled to go on.

I walked down Broughton Street to Bellevue and then to Warriston where I picked up the Water of Leith, the little river that winds its way through Edinburgh and ends up in the Forth. It'll never be talked about in the same breath as the Thames or the Seine, or even the

Clyde, but it's a smashing little brook that looks like it would fit right in to the lush, mountainy woodland of Marin county across the Bay from San Francisco.

I walked along Warriston Road, past the Lady Haig artificial poppy factory and past Powderhall dog track. Wild radish and loosestrife covered the far bank. Giant manroot, heads larger than cauliflowers, towering chestnuts and London planes had nearly reclaimed an abandoned graveyard near the DIY store. From here the river meanders into Leith. I took the footpath over the small meadow. On the way, I passed an old man picking blackberries. I said hello, but he ignored me. I walked on, stopping several times to admire the lavender thistle and snowy mespil with its small tomato-like fruit. Okay, so I used to belong to the Sierra Club.

Both the river and the landscape take a turn for the worse as you approach the docks. Before, where the water was swift, shallow and vital, it becomes still, grey, and dead. And the rustic solitude that accompanies the Water of Leith almost all the way from its headwaters in the Pentlands is broken by the sounds and sights of industry. There was a relentless hammering sound coming from somewhere nearby. The sound of giant fans, belts and machinery was even closer. The river emerges from between trees and buildings into an open area of old, dirty, brick buildings with broken windows and new office blocks and factories that look like they were designed by the geezer who built the Barbican in London. A lone seagull flew overhead.

The river widens considerably as it reaches Great Junction Street, one of the main streets in dockside Leith. Most of the area is grotty, run-down and out of date. Like an old-age pensioner down on his luck. Half the buildings look abandoned and the other half look like they should be. Faded lettering on a dilapidated building at Coalhill and Tolbooth Wynd advertises wholesale something. Exactly what belongs to history.

But like a lot of places in big city America, things in Leith are changing. Yuppie bars and restaurants are starting to sprout. And there is a very expensive-looking block of middle-class flats going up right next to the river.

The riverside pathway becomes a street near the condo construction site. I took it and continued toward the entrance to the Port of Edinburgh. On my left, the stagnant, polluted river. On my right, interrupting the depressingly grey architecture, the large black-and-red Dragon Fountain Cantonese Restaurant. It has a large gaudy gold-and-red sign that runs nearly the length of the building. Below the sign, at the corner of the building, is a smaller sign that reads "Manhattan Disco".

Men in blue overalls were returning to work from nearby dockside cafes. They were all walking in the direction of the stone portal that is the entrance to the docks. I fell in with them. Once inside, I wandered about for twenty minutes through the maze of brick roads, water slips, buildings and large cargo cranes. There was an occasional ship or two. A small freighter, an oil tanker and a mid-size passenger liner called the *Patagonian Princess*.

The gangplank was down on the South American ship so I figured I should attempt to board it. Two men at the bottom of the ramp had other ideas.

"Excuse me, sir," said one of them in thickly accented English. His posture and starched white uniform made him look taller than he really was. The silver, reflecting-lens sun-glasses made him look evil. Hopefully, more evil than he really was. "Are you a passenger?" he asked, in a manner that indicated he was reasonably sure of the answer.

"Que?" I replied in my best Spanish. I may have grown

39

up in the suburbs, but San Francisco is a very Latinized area. Six years of Spanish in school and two summers in Mexico left me sounding a lot like a native. That is, maybe to someone from South America I might sound like a Mexican. Or vice versa. Anyway, it seemed to work. I told him that I wasn't a passenger, but a friend of one of the passengers, a Miss Fuentes, who had invited me to a cocktail party on board ship. I figured there must always be at least one cocktail party in progress at any given time aboard a cruise ship. It's probably a natural law. Whatever it was, the guard seemed to have no trouble with my story. In fact, when I admitted that I wasn't too sure where Miss Fuentes' party was convening, he offered two possible locations complete with directions. I thanked him and bounced up the ramp to the promenade deck of the *Patagonian Princess*.

I wandered around for ten minutes or so casing the joint. There were a lot of people walking the decks, sunning themselves in chairs and sipping mixed drinks. Mostly older people who were generally overdressed, and young, international-set types with designer hair — who were generally underdressed.

I tried to look like I belonged on a luxury cruise ship. It wasn't easy. I was wearing brown corduroy trousers where there should have been white linen. And a raggedy pullover where there should've been a silk shirt open to the navel. And you could forget the hair. If it was designer hair, Phyllis Diller did the designing. But I've seen a couple episodes of "The Love Boat" in my time, so I wasn't a total wally.

I worked my way below deck to what looked like the crew's quarters. Looked pretty comfortable. I figured it to be the officers' digs. I know it wasn't a passenger area because the last door I passed through had the words "Restricted Entry" stencilled on it in three languages.

I passed a couple of cabins before I was met by two

middle-aged men wearing crisp officer-whites. They stopped in front of me and began speaking in Spanish. I stopped, listed a little to one side and addressed them in very American English.

"Ahoy there, mateys," I slurred. "Shiver me timbers, lads. Could you direct me to the poop deck?" I covered my mouth and giggled.

One of the officers, still speaking Spanish, spat a mild oath at me and demanded to know what I was doing in a restricted area.

"No habla the lingo, José." I said, reaching for the wall for support.

"You are in a restricted area, senor," said the other officer in perfect English. There was diplomacy in his voice.

I squinted my eyes like I was trying to focus them and turned my head from side to side. "You mean this ain't where the party is?"

"I am afraid you have lost your way, senor," said the diplomatic one. "This is where the crew lives. Passengers are not permitted in this area."

"Well, that lets me out, amigo. I'm not a passenger. I was invited to a cocktail party somewhere on this barge and I can't find it for the life of me. And I've just got to find it. They told me I could score all the snow I wanted there." I reached into my pocket and pulled out a thin roll of folded notes from my wallet. I made sure they both saw the fifty pound note on top. In the States I always carried a hundred dollar bill folded around my money. I never spent it, but it got me into more places and bought more information than all but the best television detectives get. And with the exception of Rockford, they're all much better dressers than me.

The other officer was not amused. He called me a name in Spanish. The diplomatic one told him to cool it and that he would personally escort me to the non-

41

existent cocktail party. His colleague was all too happy to be rid of me. He shot me a glance intended to shrink my skin and pushed past me on his way to somewhere more important.

The diplomatic one held out his hand and pointed in the direction I had originally come from. "This way, senor," he said. "We do not want to be late for your party."

"Fuck the party!" I said, sounding like a belligerent drunk. "I want to score some damn nose. Hell, José, I got the dough." I began to reach into my pocket again.

The diplomatic one gently grabbed my wrist. "That won't be necessary, senor." He sounded so reassuring.

We walked a few more yards and had just about reached the double doors that led to the passenger section of the ship, when my escort placed his hand on my shoulder and briskly hustled me into a small room off the corridor. The room was empty except for a small cot and table. The only thing on the table was an ashtray chock-full of long, thin, filtered butts from the kind of cigarettes a woman might smoke.

"Senor," he said. "Perhaps it is none of my business, but I am acquainted with a man who might be able to accommodate your needs."

"Needs? What are you talking about, amigo?"

"The, uh, party-needs you spoke of a moment ago."

"You mean the coke? You can get me some?"

The officer put his hand over my mouth. "Please, senor, not so loud."

"Sorry," I whispered. "But you can get me some flake, right? Some good ole nose whisky?"

"No, not me personally. But there is a man who happens to be on this ship who can supply your every need."

"A crew member?"

"I couldn't say, senor. But I hear that he is reliable."

"Say no more, José." I elbowed him in the ribs.

"Mum's the word. Now where can I meet this associate of yours? I want to score the stuff pronto."

"You must go up to the main lounge. It is on 'C' deck. A man will contact you there and tell you the time and place where the transaction will be conducted."

"How will I know him?"

"Don't worry, senor. He will know you."

"Okay, José. You got yourself a deal. But I'll tell you I'm not going to wait around up there all day. You dig?"

"Thirty minutes, my friend. A man will contact you within thirty minutes."

"Well, bueno. I'll be there." The officer then ushered me out of the room. It had all taken about a minute. "Say, captain," I said, as he opened the door to the non-restricted world. "Who owns this tub?"

"Senor?"

"The *Patagonian Princess*. Where does she hail from?"

"We are sailing under the flag of Chile, senor."

"Muchas graziano." Somewhere between the "muchas" and the "graziano", I found myself on the other side of the double doors. Alone.

I had been in the 'C' deck lounge for about fifteen minutes listening to some salsa being piped over the sound system and sucking a tequila sunrise when a short, dark man in a white line suit and an open-necked shirt with orange, purple and green orchids printed on a bright red background slid into the chair next to me.

He spoke to me while looking at something else. "Calton Hill. The monument. Eleven-thirty tonight. Bring cash." It was more like a telegram than the beginning of a conversation. Before I could send a reply he got up and walked away like he had never been there.

A man of few words, that one. But those few words said a lot. Like linking Rodrigo Perez with the international narcotics trade. It was likely both were in the same part of Calton Hill the night of the murder. Some coincidence, eh?

I would have left the *Patagonian Princess* at that point and gone home to break the news to Morag that the great revolutionary playwright was most likely wasted by the South American drug mafia. And that would've been that. Nobody in their right mind would have expected me, or anyone else for that matter, to do anything more.

But my curiosity demanded that I do one more thing. I worked my way back down to the deck where the officers' quarters were located. There was something about that little room the diplomatic officer shoved me into. Something about the cigarette butts in the ashtray. Like, what were women's cigarette stumps doing in the officers' quarters? The easy answer was they were put there by female officers. But a couple things didn't fit. First, they were all the same brand, which indicated they were smoked by the same person. And second, there were a lot of them and no signs that any other life existed in that tiny compartment. That suggested that a single person, a woman, was in that room for a long time. Waiting for someone? Or maybe being kept by someone.

I found the door again that said "Restricted Entry" and pushed it open. The second door on my right was the entrance to the tiny room full of cigarette butts. The door was locked, but a little device that I always carry on my person, one that is definitely not sold in the shops, found the lock to be very obliging.

The room looked pretty much the same as before except the ashtray was gone. I walked over to a door located at the rear of the cabin. I hadn't noticed it before. I reached into my pocket for my tool and was about to apply it to the lock when the door opened.

The short, dark man in the linen suit and technicolour shirt was standing in the doorway. There was a gun in his hand and a look in his eyes that told me he had used it before. He also looked like the kind of guy who wouldn't fall for the lost-drunk routine.

We stood face-to-face for a moment that seemed long enough to re-edit the Oxford Dictionary. In that time I knew I wasn't going to be able to talk my way out.

"You will step inside," said the man with the gun.

"Does this mean I don't get the coke?"

"Inside!" He waved the gun angrily and started to back slowly into the room. He motioned to me to follow him. "Very slowly," he said.

I took one slow step and then another. Before I took a third I grabbed the half-open door by the knob and slammed it shut with a swiftness that surprised even me.

There I was. The short, dark man with the gun was on one side of the door and I was on the other. I could live with that arrangement, but I knew he couldn't. So, I turned and ran as fast as my fleshy legs would carry me. I hadn't reached the outer door that opened to the corridor before I heard his gun go off. I could almost feel the business end of the bullet thud into the wall near my head.

I dived into the corridor, rolled over once and sprung to my feet. I was through the restricted entry doors and up to the passenger deck in less time than it takes an anorexic teenager to eat supper. I didn't even know if the short, dark man and his gun were in pursuit.

I reached the ramp that connected the ship with the dock, stopped and looked around. No one in a technicolour shirt shooting at me. I tucked in my shirt and walked down the ramp like I had just won the jackpot in a shuffleboard tournament. I didn't even look back. But I knew what was there. Somewhere on board. A cocaine dealer with a gun. That and a woman I saw lying on a cot in the room that contained the cocaine dealer and his gun. A woman who looked a lot like the press photos of the widow of Rodrigo Perez.

CHAPTER EIGHT

When I hit the docks I began running and didn't stop until I reached an uptown bus stop. I caught the first one that came. I couldn't help thinking, as the coach bounced up Leith Walk, that I was really in the soup. Like over my head. It was bad enough that I slammed a door in the face of a mafia gunman, but I got away from him. Bad guys hate that. And if that weren't enough for a stonemason to start chisling me a tombstone, I saw something I wasn't supposed to see. Something I wished I hadn't seen. Something that geezers like the man in the rainbow shirt with the gun could quite possibly interpret as a capital offence. Something that made me wish I was out of town. Maybe this was a good time to begin tracing my roots in old Italy. Frosinone, was it?

All of these things raced through my mind as the bus climbed the slope leading to Princes Street. I got off near North Bridge, then walked down the Waverley Steps, through the train station and out the other side to the City Arts Centre Cafe. I needed a cappuccino bad. I ordered same, and a shortbread. I slid my tray along to the cash register. Helen was in the kitchen. She saw me and waved. I waved back. I reached into my pocket for my wallet to pay for my food. It wasn't there. A sweat colder than a penguin's ankles broke out on my forehead. It wasn't simply the kind of sweat that said thieves were now in possession of your credit cards and are at this very moment running up a five thousand pound tab in your name at Marks and Spencer. No, it was a cold sweat that said the man with the gun knows your name, where you live, what colour eyes you have and how much you weigh. Could be fatal information. For me. And for Morag! I raced out of the cafe to the nearest phone and dialled her number. Our number. There was no answer.

For the first time since arriving in Edinburgh, I took

a cab. It took less than ten minutes to reach the flat. Seven-and-a-half to be exact. Thirty-two since I left the company of the short, dark man and his gun.

I raced up the stairs to the flat. The door was open. I called out Morag's name, which might not have been the smartest thing to do. I called out again, this time announcing that I had called the police and that they would be here in two minutes. Works sometimes on "The Rockford Files". But, then, Sergeant Becker and the LAPD usually *were* only two minutes away.

I stood outside the door for another fifteen seconds or so before finally going inside. It's a small flat so it didn't take long to find Morag. She was lying on the kitchen floor. The chairs were overturned and dishes were broken and scattered all over the place. Lillian was standing stiffly in a corner.

It looked like Morag had put up a fight. I knew she would. I hoped the man in the orchid shirt had paid a price for his assault. The left side of Morag's face was swollen and covered with freshly dried blood. I bent down and felt for a pulse on her wrist. A slow, but rhythmic beating let me know she was alive, if only just. I called for an ambulance and applied cold compresses to her head until it arrived.

I rode with her to the Royal Infirmary. I held her limp hand all the way to the emergency room. Fat lot of good that did for either one of us. She couldn't feel it and I couldn't forget it. Forget that my carelessness and stupidity had put her there. Memories of that last case in Frisco pushed their way into the screening room of my mind. I relived once again the terrible shooting on Bryant Street and the woman slipping from my arms as she fell under an assassin's bullet. The shock and surprise on her face. That was the worst part. She seemed to be saying, "But you promised me everything was going to be alright. I trusted you."

47

I sat in the waiting room for hours. Well past the time Mark Miwurdz went on at the Assembly Rooms. Around ten-thirty, a doctor came out and told me that Morag had suffered a concussion, but that there didn't appear to be any signs of brain damage. He said he would know more when she regained consciousness which wouldn't be for another twelve hours or so. The fact that she was alive and had a good chance of pulling through should have cheered me. It did some. But all I could think of was that I was the kind of guy who should have learned to say "no" to people a long time ago. It could have saved a lot of pain all around.

CHAPTER NINE

There was no way I could stay at my flat. To do so would have been an advert for another brain concussion. Mine. So I called Annie. I met Annie a couple of months after coming to Edinburgh, at a public Socialist Workers' Party meeting where Paul Foot spoke about the miners' strike. She has red hair, a few freckles near her nose and a reasonably good sense of humour. She does something for the SWP, but I have never been exactly sure just what. Anyway, we see each other regularly. When she isn't organizing SWP discos, or I'm not out roaming the moors in some kind of self-imposed existential trance, trying to force the muses to inspire me to write the "Great American Novel", which I and thousands, if not millions, of Americans are convinced lurk somewhere deep within our breasts.

I hadn't seen Annie for almost a week. The last time was at Marty's Grill in the Haymarket where we had another row over the SWP's position on the Labour party. I got so steamed I couldn't even finish my apple blunder.

She wasn't too pleased when I phoned at 11:30, but softened up a whole lot when I told her what happened to Morag. She and Morag had been friends at university. In fact, it was Morag who introduced me to Annie at the Paul Foot meeting.

Annie wanted to come to the hospital right away to be with Morag, but I told her she couldn't have visitors and wouldn't be conscious until morning at least. She agreed reluctantly to let me come over and spend the night.

I walked from the hospital to Annie's place. It wasn't far. Just on the other side of the Meadows. When I got there the kettle was on the boil. Annie looked to be nearly overcome with anxiety. About Morag.

Over a cup of tea and a plate of biscuits and cold toast I told Annie everything that had happened to me since reading the article about the Perez murder earlier in the day. She remained silent throughout my recapitulation, only interrupting to ask for elaboration or clarification. When I finished, I rolled my shoulders and said,"So, where do I go from here?"

Annie took a bite of toast. "If I were you, I'd go as far away from here as possible. You could stay with my sister on Skye."

"Not with Morag lying in hospital with a broken head. I may not have many principles left, but I can't just walk away from this without doing something. Someone's going to have to pay for it."

"How? You're not exactly the head of an organization that can have a fracas with the drug mafia and live to tell the tale."

There was no denying that. I mean, after the row I had with Annie at Marty's, I wasn't even sure I could count on moral support from here.

"I can't just run away from it," I said. "And I can't forget it. I know too much and they know I know too much. That doesn't leave me many options, does it?"

"What would Rockford do in this situation?" Annie said. She wasn't laughing.

"Are you making fun of me?"

"Ach, no. I'm trying to help."

"Do you think I could get any help from the SWP?"

This time she laughed. "Are you daft? What kind of help? We may have fought the National Front, but this is a bit different. Why don't you ask your pals in the Labour Party?"

"You *are* making fun of me."

"Sorry. I thought you were joking. To be honest, about the only thing the party could do in this situation is to organize a jumble sale to raise money to pay for your funeral."

"Thanks. That's the kind of encouragement I was looking for."

"Well, what did you expect? There are only two forces in this part of the world that I know of can take on the mafia. The IRA and the miners."

"Hmmm."

"I still think you should go to Skye for a while. Until things cool down."

"No, you're right. The only thing to do is follow this thing through."

"What?"

"Just taking your advice, hen."

"You're a bampot. You know that? What in the world are you talking about?"

"That's what Rockford would do. Follow it through. At least till the end of the episode." I laughed through my nose. "Look. If nothing else, I've uncovered a narcotics ring that's operating right off the *Patagonian Princess*. That should interest somebody in this town. Maybe somebody in the Labour majority on the Disrict Council."

"Oh, aye. The Labour Party will take on the drug

mafia just for you. They've been looking for a hot issue ever since their rate-capping campaign fell through."

"You laugh."

"I'm not laughing, Rocco."

"Look. In addition to that, I saw Lily Montevideo, right? The cops are looking for her. I could toss her right into their laps."

"The joke would be on you if she wasn't really kidnapped. You said yourself it was a possibility. I don't think the drug traffickers, the police or the Chileans would be terribly chuffed if they were all involved in this together. It might just get you into more trouble. Then where would you be? I'd really suggest Skye as a more reasonable alternative."

Annie had a good point. These international socialists are so dialectical. Drawing attention to myself was the last thing I should do. Going to the police would just about put me on page one. No, there was a lot more to this than a simple old-fashioned case of underworld crime. Going to Skye was a seductive idea. I've only seen the Cuillens once before and that was at dusk. But a couple of weeks or months in Portree, where Annie's sister lives, wouldn't have answered any questions about Lily Montevideo. Besides, with Morag lying in hospital, I felt like I owed her something more than running away.

It was late. Mark Miwurdz and the political cabaret had been over for hours. Even the late-night cabaret at the Fringe Club was probably beginning to wind down. I smoked a cigarette while sucking on a mint humbug. Annie was fading. She got up from her chair, took my hand and led me into the bedroom. There for the next twenty minutes I thought only about the good things in life. My life. The beauty of the peaks and the moors in the highlands, cappuccinos at the City Art Centre, Sergeant Bilko back on BBC2, the Water of Leith and walks in the Pentlands. And, of course, Annie. After that everything was blank until Annie woke me the next morning.

CHAPTER TEN

Annie was gone by the time I finally got out of bed. Gone to work. To the print shop in Fountainbridge where she sets type and operates an offset press. One of us has to work and I'm almost always glad it's her. But now I had work, too. Staying healthy was a big part of the job description.

I was out of Annie's flat by nine. I crossed the Meadows and was at the Royal Infirmary fifteen minutes later. The doctor told me Morag had regained consciousness, but was still in danger. He said there were some additional tests to be run on her before he could be any more definite. I wanted to look in on her, but he told me she was under sedation. He said I could stop back later in the afternoon.

I hiked down George IV Bridge to the Royal Mile. I stopped at the Fringe Office to pick up another Fringe Guide. In front of the office, four young women in tap shoes, dressed like tarted-up dance hall girls, were dancing and singing a song about breasts while two others passed out leaflets to the stream of people passing by. I took one. It announced an afternoon perfomance by the Darlettes who were doing a satirical musical revue called "Tits and Brits."

A couple of geezers in black trousers held up by braces, and wearing black and white striped shirts stood a few yards away juggling knives and oranges.

I elbowed my way into the small Fringe headquarters, picked up my guide and elbowed my way back outside.

The Darlettes were gone. A young man wearing an enormous sandwich-board that announced everything you would ever need to know about the productions of a Cambridge theatre group, clomped up the street toward the Lawnmarket.

Given the past twenty-four hours, a Fringe Guide was probably the last thing in the world I needed, but you've got to be optimistic about these things.

I took my Fringe Guide and walked down the Royal Mile to Cockburn Street and then down Fleshmarket Steps to the City Art Centre. Helen was behind the counter slicing freshly baked shortbread into generous rectangles.

"Good morning, Rocco," she said looking up from her work as I picked up a tray from the stack at the end of the food service table.

"Let's hope so," I said eyeing the trays of shortbread.

"The usual for you this morning?"

"And how. Wait. Better make that two pieces of shortbread to go with the cappuccino. I'm going to need all the sugar I can ingest."

Helen put the shortbread on a plate and handed it to me over the glass food case. "See any good shows last night?" she asked.

"Naw. I was up with a sick friend."

"Nothing serious, I hope."

"Remind me to tell you about it when everything gets back to normal." I tilted my head to the long line of customers that was forming up behind me.

"Aye," she said, putting the last of the shortbread onto the glass shelves. "It'll be like this until the Chinese Warriors leave town."

I smiled. If I didn't know she meant the exhibition at the Art Centre I might have imagined angry Red Guards waving Mao's little red book. Or Oriental youth gangs steeped in martial arts. Or maybe a touring football team from Beijing."

Helen then made my cappuccino and rung everything up at the cash register. "If you want a good laugh," she said, "you should go see the Bodgers. They're at the Pleasance. I saw them last night. They're great fun."

I nodded and made a mental note to add the Bodgers to my list of things to see. I paid for my food and took a table at the far corner of the cafe. Jimmy came in a few minutes later with *The Scotsman*. I bought one. The Perez murder was still front-page news, but there didn't appear there was much new to report. The article said the police had no leads concerning the whereabouts of Lily Montevideo and they were fearing the worst. So was I. About a lot of things.

I got this uncomfortable feeling that someone was reading the paper over my shoulder. I looked up and turned in my chair to see a tall man wearing silver reflecting-lens sun-glasses standing over me. It was the ramp guard from the *Patagonian Princess*. I had the feeling he hadn't stopped by for rolls and coffee. He looked like he wasn't in the mood for my Mexican Spanish, either.

"Senor," he said, in a quiet, even voice. "You will please come with me."

I took a sip of my cappuccino. "Where's that?" I asked.

"Some people would like to speak with you."

"Can't you see I'm having my breakfast? Why don't you just leave me their phone number and I'll call them later."

"I have my instructions to bring you with me, senor."

"I don't want you to take this personally, but suppose I don't want to go with you?"

"I am afraid there is little choice, senor." The man unbuttoned his suit jacket to reveal the butt of a revolver

54

tucked into the waistband of his pants. It illustrated just how little choice I had.

"You wouldn't use that thing in here," I said. It sounded almost like a question.

"I would not want to find out if I were you."

I popped the last bite of shortbread into my mouth and took a final swallow from my cup. "Well, what are we waiting for?" The man in the sun-glasses smiled slightly.

We walked out of the cafe to Market Street. "Which way?" I asked.

"Please cross the street."

"Sure. I looked down the street. An *Evening News* lorry had just turned the corner at Waverley onto the cobblestones of Market Street.

"Senor," said the man in the sun-glasses, placing his hand in the middle of my back.

I began to step off the curb. I let *The Scotsman*, that I was carrying under my arm fall to the pavement. "Ooops!" I said. I started to bend down to pick it up.

"Leave the paper," the man in the sun-glasses said. I could tell he was beginning to lose his patience.

Hey! I haven't played today's Investor game." I went down for the paper on one knee. "You should get a card. You could win a thousand pounds, you know."

"Senor! You are wasting time." He put his hand on my elbow to help me up.

I placed the ball of my right foot against the curb and pushed off with everything I had, just as the *Evening News* lorry was speeding past. I beat it by a split second as it jammed on its brakes and came to a screeching halt. The man in the sun-glasses wasn't so lucky. I didn't look back until I reached the Market Street entrance to the train station. I did hear the irate driver of the lorry yell out, "Bloody English bastard!". How was he to know?

I ran down the corridor that crossed over the tracks. As I reached the steps that led down to the platform I turned and saw the man in the sun-glasses. He wasn't far behind me and his gun was drawn.

I scrambled down the steps and dived for the first cab in line, pushing away a middle-aged couple who had that tasteless, but expensive, American Sun Belt look.

"Where to, mate?" said the cabbie out of the corner of his mouth.

"Outta here!" I shouted from the floor of his hack. "And don't spare the nags."

"The what?"

"Step on it, for chrissakes! Move! Move!"

The cab shot up the loop road and onto the street. Five minutes later we were in the Haymarket. I had the cab let me out in front of Marty's Grill. There I had a steamed coffee and a bacon roll while trying to put myself back together and resist the overwhelming urge to get the next coach to Skye.

Not only did the bad guys know my name, address, height, weight and colour of eyes, but also the places where I hang out. This was becoming personal and I didn't like it.

CHAPTER ELEVEN

Following my snack at Marty's, I took another cab to George Street. The George Hotel. I checked with the front-desk man. Yes, he told me, Teatro Jara were still in residence. I hiked up to the third floor to the Perez suite.

It was some time before my knock was answered. The door was opened by a large, stocky woman wearing a green pendleton shirt, blue jeans and Doc Martin boots. She had short blonde hair and a scowl on her face.

"Yeah?" She spat the word out of the side of her

mouth like it was tobacco juice. It wasn't particularly nasty, the way she said it. I figured it was just her way of saying "Hi".

"I'd like to see Pete Swallow," I said.

"You and about a thousand other people." She was American.

"I have some information about Lily Montevideo."

The woman's eyes squinted like she was experiencing a migraine headache. "Yeah, that's what they all say."

"No, really. I know where she is."

"Tell me," she insisted.

"I'll tell Pete Swallow."

"You one of the goddamn kidnappers, man?" Before I could explain myself, she reached out and grabbed my shirt and pulled. Two buttons popped right away. The others strained against the material, making the holes larger.

"Hey!" I shouted. She twisted her fist, which pulled my shirt even tighter. The collar was choking me. I swung up, hitting her forearm with my fist. It was hard enough to break her grip. She stepped back and squared off like she would plant her fist in my face if I gave her half an excuse.

An arm draped in a black satin robe reached over her shoulder. "What's going on here, Michelle?" its owner demanded to know.

Michelle relaxed her stance and turned to the man behind her. "This fuckhead says he knows where Lily is."

The man eased Michelle out of the doorway. "Is that any reason to create a scene?" The man smiled and looked at me. "Please come in, Mr, uh . . ."

"The name's Conigliaro."

"And mine is Pete Swallow."

I walked into the room. Michelle backed inside never taking her eyes from me. I followed Swallow into the

57

sitting area of the suite. He gestured for me to sit down. I did. He sat opposite me in the stuffed mohair. He crossed his legs. I lit a smoke.

Everything about him was "ish". Tallish, fiftyish. Hair greyish and skin palish. Very English, I thought.

"Please forgive Michelle," he said, in a voice that only suggested sincerity. "With all that has happened, you really can't blame her for not trusting anyone."

It was my popped buttons I blamed her for, not her lack of trust. "Who is she, anyway?" I asked, looking around to make sure she wasn't preparing to rush me from behind. She was standing next to the large fireplace in the corner of the room.

"Michelle is our security person," said Swallow.

"Oh. She on holiday?" It was a bad joke in bad taste. I was in a bad mood. I turned quickly in my chair. Michelle started toward me. Her face was taut and angry. I stood up.

Swallow clapped his hands together. "Michelle! Please! Leave us alone for a while. Why don't you go down to the bar and have yourself a drink."

Michelle was stopped by Swallow's words, but she wasn't through with me. She jabbed a finger at me the way baseball managers do at umpires when they are having a fist-class rhubarb. "We're goin' to go some heads, asshole," she said. "Just you and me. Ya dig?"

"Michelle!" Swallow shouted. He stood up and pointed to the door. "Please! The bar!"

"Fuck you too, man!" she said. She stood looking at us for a long moment. Then she hitched up her pants. "I'll be down in the bar, then."

Swallow laughed nervously. "She's really taking this very hard," he said. "She was very devoted to Rodrigo and Lily. Very devoted. She had been with them longer than any of us. But we are all terribly upset, as you might well imagine. I've had to make all the funeral

58

arrangements. It has been a ghastly experience, I don't mind telling you. Rodrigo was so full of life. So vital. So, so here!" Swallow turned his head away from me. He made a small fist and put it up to his mouth and bit one of his knuckles. Tears came to his eyes.

"Yes, he will be missed by a lot of people," I said.

"There will never be another Rodrigo Perez. Just like there will never be another Shakespeare or another Brecht. They were geniuses, who come along once every few generations. They are like comets. They give off great heat and illuminate the heavens with their presence. Then puff, they are gone. It is sad, so truly sad, don't you think?"

I did, but I hadn't come to chat about the cosmological importance of Rodrigo Perez. I was more interested in the earthly presence of Lily Montevideo. I told Swallow I had seen the missing actress.

"Where?" he said, almost breathlessly. "How is she? Is she alright? Did you tell the police? Why didn't she come with you? Did she say anything about me?" The questions were as fast as cricket balls on a test-match wicket in the heat of the midday sun. I couldn't answer most of them and wasn't sure I wanted to answer the other. I was the detective here. I was the one who was supposed to ask the questions.

I told him that I had seen her in the cabin and presence of a no-nonsense narcotics trafficker. I told him I saw her for only a brief moment and that was from a distance. She was reclining on a cot. She looked to be in the room of her own free-will, but then again, I only got a glimpse. I suppose she could have been drugged. It was a possibility.

Swallow liked that possibility. He could live with it. Run with it. "That must be it!" he said, clasping his hands together. "The drug traffickers killed Rodrigo and kidnapped Lily and then took her to the boat. We must telephone the police." He rose from his chair and began walking towards the phone.

"Hold on!" I said, stopping him before he reached it. "Just suppose for a moment that Lily isn't kidnapped."

"That's preposterous!" He picked up the receiver.

"But if she isn't, or she is drugged to say she isn't, telling the cops will only muck things up. It might get both of you more trouble than you can handle. The police don't understand things like that. They might fit up the both of you for the murder. And besides, the drug mafiosi play rough. We bring the cops down on them they're likely to start measuring us for lead kilts, if you know what I mean. In fact, I forgot to mention, that's just about what happened to me on my way over here."

"You're joking!" Swallow forgot about the phone call and returned to his chair. He took a long, slim, filtered cigarette from a small wooden box on the coffee table in front of him. He lit it with a lighter he produced from a pocket in his robe.

"You've been threatened?" he said, filling the immediate area around him with exhaled smoke.

"That's how I interpreted it."

"It's damnable!" he said, raising his voice. Actually, I thought it was a whole lot worse than damnable. "What do they want with Lily?" he continued. "Why would they want to kill poor Rodrigo?" The questions were more rhetorical than anything else. I sure didn't have the answers.

I talked with Swallow for another forty-five minutes. A lot of it was about what a swell guy Rodrigo Perez was and his place in the history of the theatre. But he could shed no light on why Perez and Montevideo were on Calton Hill at midnight other than to say they liked to take walks at night. He was also no help in establishing a connection between Perez and the narcotics traffickers. When I told him they were both Chilean he gulped, but

60

couldn't offer anything more than personal speculation. He swore that both Perez and Montevideo were not drug users. An occasional marijuana joint, but nothing more potent. It was one blind alley after another. He even claimed he didn't know Morag. Then the conversation turned to the play, *Ships in the Night*.

"Why was last night's opening postponed?" I asked.

Swallow recrossed his legs and lit another cigarette from the small wooden box. "That is not easy to say," he said, after a lengthy pause. "For one thing it wasn't really ready."

"That's strange, isn't it? A pro like Perez not being ready. You mean the actors hadn't learned all their lines?"

Swallow chuckled. "No. The difficulties were a little more complicated than that."

"I'm listening."

"We were having political troubles. I guess it's all right to be telling you this. The government threatened to deport Rodrigo unless they were provided with a copy of the script in advance of the play's opening. Well, of course, Rodrigo refused to comply. The Home Office followed by initiating deportation proceedings against him. They also informed the management of the Assembly Rooms that they would not allow the play to open if Rodrigo didn't allow them the opportunity to review the script and approve it. We only found this out last week."

"And Perez still wouldn't cooperate, right?"

"Rodrigo refused to be censored. He said that was the reason he was in exile from fascist Chile. He held a press conference three days ago in London to explain his position. He compared Thatcher to Pinochet and said the only difference he could see between Britain and Chile was that Chile had better food. After that the Home Office turned up the heat on both the Assembly Rooms and the members of the company. The night before last, Kate Wallace, one of the actresses in the company, told us she'd been threatened and was leaving the production."

"Threatened by who? The Home Office?"

"She didn't know. Or wouldn't tell us. But it was obvious that it was being orchestrated by the government. Anyway, Kate said the only way she would stay was if Rodrigo would give the script to the Home Office. They had a furious row over it. Kate was new to the company and didn't have the political commitment of the others. Her commitment was to her career and she didn't see the harm in cooperating with the government. Rodrigo stood firm and refused to give in. To anybody. It was a matter of principle with him. Just about everything was a matter of principle with Rodrigo."

"You make it sound like maybe that wasn't such a good thing."

Swallow stood up and re-wrapped his robe. "Not at all. I just hated to see Kate and Rodrigo rowing, that's all. It was bad for the morale of the company. It was the last thing we needed at that point." Swallow was standing behind his chair leaning on it with outstretched hands.

"So, what happened to this Kate Wallace?" I asked.

"She left the show."

"When?"

"Yesterday."

"Where did she go?"

Swallow shrugged his shoulders. "Back to London, I suppose. I really don't know. She lives somewhere in Paddington."

"But you're not sure where she went?"

"No. I am not sure where she went. Is it important?"

"I don't know. Did the Home Office put the screws to anyone else or was Kate the only one?"

"Oh, they tried to get to the others, but Kate was the

only one who cracked. Like I said she didn't have the commitment of the others. I don't know, maybe they had something nasty on her and used it to get her to wreck the production."

"You mean blackmail?"

"Well, it has happened before. You see, the Home Office is used to having its own way. When Rodrigo refused to give the Home Office a copy of the script they began harassing members of the company. Kate was the weak link in an otherwise solid chain. We all knew that. I guess you might even say the row between her and Rodrigo was inevitable."

"This may sound stupid, but why didn't Wallace just give the Home Office her own script? She had one, didn't she?"

"Ah. This is where it gets tricky. Normally, yes, she would have had a script, as would the rest of the cast and the stage manager. But because of the political sensitivity of the play, Rodrigo kept them all under lock and key. And when rehearsals were far enough along, he destroyed them. I personally helped him burn them in the fireplace at the school."

"I see. This guy wasn't taking any chances, was he?"

"He was even more cautious than that. He thought spies might try to bug the rehearsals in order to electronically reproduce the script."

"That must've been a real possibility."

"It most certainly was. That's why in even full rehearsals certain sections of the play were never spoken aloud."

"Sort of makes it tough to rehearse, doesn't it?"

"Rodrigo, you see, had structured the play in such a manner that at certain points in the script, he would deliver substantial monologues. No one ever heard these because they were cut from the rehearsal and didn't appear in any of the written scripts. Rodrigo said the monologues contained the politically sensitive material and if their content were known, the government would never allow the play to open."

"And that material died with him on Calton Hill?"

"I admit it was foolish of him to be there last night. Or any night from what I have subsequently heard about the place. But Rodrigo was no fool. He knew his life was at risk. It was an occupational hazard given the political content of his work."

"What are you driving at?"

"There is a script. A single script with everything in it."

"Including the monologues?"

"Everything. Rodrigo wanted the information to survive even if he didn't. I think he knew there would be attempts on his life."

"So, where is this script?"

Swallow shrugged his shoulders. "That, my friend, is a very good question. I think Lily knows, but she would be the only one."

"And, of course, if anything happens to her . . ."

"That would be the end of *Ships in the Night*. At least as Rodrigo would have wanted it. With the monologues."

"Do you have any idea as to what was in them?"

"Well, as you might have read, the subject-matter of the play was the sinking of the *General Belgrano*."

"Yeah, that's no secret."

"But there was another theme that was not well known to the public. The secret agreement between Britain and Chile during the Falklands."

"Chile?"

"Yes. It was written up by Duncan Campbell in the *New Statesman* some time ago. Pinochet provided Thatcher with a secret air base at Puenta Arenas and a free exchange of intelligence including the monitoring and code breaking of Argentine signals carried out by

Chilean Naval Intelligence staff. In return, Maggie gave Pinochet some Canberras and a squadron of Hawker Hunters and promised to help him block the UN from its human rights investigations in Chile. She also promised to drop British restrictions on arms sale to the Pinochet regime."

"I guess I missed that issue of the *Statesman*."

"Rodrigo went further than the *New Statesman* revelations. Much further. Both factually and creatively. However, he would only tell me that it was a hot pistol and that it could bring Thatcher to her knees. That's what he said. He told me what he had was a clear violation of the Official Secrets Act and would make the trial of Clive Ponting look like an afternoon on the lawn at Wimbledon."

"And Lily Montevideo is the only person who knows where this script is, right?"

"As far as I know she is. Rodrigo was a much adored man, but he didn't have many friends. Friends he could trust implicitly, that is."

"What about you? I thought you were his right-hand man."

Swallow looked away. He took another cigarette from the wooden box and lit it up. "I was closer to Rodrigo than anyone in the company. Maybe anyone in Britain. Excluding Lily, of course. But, as I said, he was a hard person to get close to. I neither sought nor expected any closer confidence with him than that which I enjoyed."

Finally, the conversation got back to Lily Montevideo. I reckoned Michelle was probably on her third pint by now and I didn't really want to be around when she returned. So I tried to be brief.

Swallow still thought the police should be called in. I had to admit that it was the most convenient thing to do. But, if DINA, as they call the secret police of Chile, *and* MI6 were involved, which was all too likely given the nature of the play's subject-matter, then the joke would be on us and we might end up like Perez. It's always so hard to play ball when the other side won't tell you the ground rules. And in this case I wasn't even sure who the other side was.

We needed to approach the situation with extreme caution. If I thought it would've worked I'd have suggested we send an unsigned note to the bad guys asking them to release Ms Montevideo, promising on a stack of Bibles that we would forget the whole thing. But I knew it wouldn't work. Too stupid. But there really didn't seem to be a whole lot of room to manoeuvre. Did we tell the police or shoot our way onto the *Patagonian Princess* like a bunch of Israeli commandos? I tried to imagine what guys like Rockford would do in this situation. Something creative and clever, that was for sure. Something Jimmy Joe Meeker-like.

I suggested to Swallow that we use our imaginations to gain access to the ship and get to Lily Montevideo. I mean, I was, after all, dealing with actors.

Swallow was for it. He insisted Michelle be included. "If for no other reason than if she finds out what we're doing and isn't included, she will be very unhappy. Besides, she knows karate."

I was in no position to disagree with him. In fact, as my nimble mind patched together possible scenarios, I thought she might work out quite well, indeed.

Swallow poured us a couple of scotches and we got down to the business of drafting a plan to rescue the actress without a whole lot of people getting killed in the process.

We had just about put the finishing touches on it when Michelle returned. She called me a few names with her eyes, but when Swallow explained the plan to her and my involvement with it, she became downright non-threatening.

CHAPTER TWELVE

An hour later I was in the parking lot in front of the Waterfront Wine Bar, a trendy pub that serves the kind of food you find in chi-chi bistros in California. I was joined by twenty other people, all called together by Peter Swallow. We were all dressed as mimes, clowns, jugglers and characters from Italian *commedia del arte*. Swallow himself was wearing a black-and-white diamond-patterned suit with slippers whose toes curved upwards into a point. He carried a wooden mitre in his hand.

Michelle was dressed in a long green velour gown trimmed with frilly white lace. Perched on her head was a tall conical hat that had a gauze scarf flowing from the point. She looked a lot like Rapunzel. And a little like Rapunzel's brother, too. I think it was the scowl she was wearing on her face and the cigarette hanging from the corner of her mouth. It made her look like a graduate from the Damon Runyon School of Tough Guys and Urban Street Characters. It was almost comical.

But if Michelle looked comical, I looked ridiculous. I was wearing maroon velvet balloon pants that came down to my knees where a pair of white stockings took over and continued south. I wore a short, one-button jacket that was cut to fit a much smaller person. On my face I wore a rubber nose that made Cyrano de Bergerac look like he had had his bobbed. It made my vision something I could no longer take for granted. It was a bit dodgy trying to see around the huge proboscis and over the thick, white accordion collar around my neck. A tiny clown hat, the kind Chico Marx used to wear, and a half-pound of pancake make-up completed an outfit that would have embarrassed my own dear mother. I had worked under cover plenty of times, but never in pantaloons and a Buster Brown jacket.

The twenty other souls were performers from various Fringe productions who were only too glad to answer the call on behalf of the late Rodrigo Perez. And that was about the extent of their knowledge of our plan. Each had an instrument or a noise-maker in addition to their costume. We looked like a bloody medieval circus.

I banged my instrument — a pair of small cymbals. — to call the troupe to order. I explained that I wanted them to sing, make noise and generally be obnoxious as we marched through the *Patagonian Princess*. I told them they were to follow the signals of Maestro Gelato, as Swallow agreed to be called, and if anyone asked we were drumming up support for Fringe Sunday in Holyrood Park, where we were to perform. And I told them we would be "I Fratelli e Sorrelle Schiavone" for the next hour or so. It was just a name that popped into my head. I don't think anyone in Edinburgh or the *Patagonian Princess* would know that it was a construction firm in New Jersey that had connections with the mob and a defrocked Reagan Secretary of Labour.

We pushed off from the parking lot and began marching through the docks towards the ship. Drums, flutes and bugles conspired to create an awful din. However, among our number were a couple musicians who took it upon themselves to lead the rest in some faintly recognizable tunes.

People stopped in their tracks to watch the spectacle. Some even smiled and waved. Had it been any time of the year other than Festival season, someone would surely have called the police. Or the public health authority.

We neared the *Patagonian Princess*. The stiff-backed geezer in the sun-glasses who had wanted to take me for a ride was standing at the bottom of the ramp. He was accompanied by another who looked like he came from the same genetic dish.

We snaked up to the ramp singing, dancing, tooting, pounding and clapping. With my false nose, hat and white face there was little chance I would be recognized. I motioned to the troupe to increase the musical tempo.

I walked up to the ramp guards. "Signori," I said. "We are 'I Fratelli e Sorrelle Schiavone'. From Firenze. In Italia."

One of the guards cupped his hand around his ear and said. "What?"

I pointed to the ship. "We have the great honour to perform our latest *commedia* for the kind passengers of your *nave*."

The same guard leaned forward and repeated himself. "What?"

The other one — the one who had wanted me to meet his friends — wasn't amused. "You must have a pass," he said firmly. "No one can board without a boarding pass."

This time it was my turn to cup my ear. "No capito, signore," I said.

Swallow came up and shook the hand of the one who was hard of hearing. "Grazie, signore," he said, grabbing the man's hand. He shook it like he was a policeman directing rush-hour traffic in Rome. "Grazie, grazie, grazie," he repeated. Then he tried to hug him, but the guard pushed him away.

"You cannot board the ship without a boarding pass," said the one in the sun-glasses. He then began pushing us away from the ramp.

Michelle burst through the crowd to the front. I clutched my cymbals. She stood directly in front of the two guards. Then she started a Salome dance right under their noses. She took a scarf from her waist and waved it around the face of the one with the sun-glasses giving him a very seductive wink as she touched his chest with her shoulder. The man leered and reached for her. I

69

held my breath. I knew if he touched her she was likely to smash his windpipe and our little diversion would be all over. But she was quick enough to jump back into the crowd of clowns and musicians before he could lay hands on her. She had played it magnificently.

I gave the signal to start up the ramp. "Avanti popolo," I said, and the twenty of us began dancing and singing our way up the ramp. One or both of the guards were shouting at us. I looked back and waved. "Ciao, amici," I said, smiling. The one with the sun-glasses took out a walkie-talkie from his belt and spoke into it.

I remembered where the main promenade deck was located. I figured there was bound to be a lot of passengers lying about on deck chairs, so I sent the troupe there with Swallow and told him to wing it until they were thrown off the ship. I took Michelle and retraced my steps to the officers' quarters.

We raced down the steps two decks to the officers' quarters. "This better not be a wild-goose chase, buster," Michelle hissed between short, quick breaths.

"Would I lie? I said back.

"For your sake, you better not be. I feel like a goddamn idiot in this fucking dress."

"Hey! You look lovely."

"Fuck you, Jack!"

We reached the double doors with the restricted entry sign on them. I pushed through. Michelle followed.

"She's in there," I said, pointing to the cabin door.

"Well, what are we waiting for, schmuck? Let's kick it in." She raised her leg into the door-smashing position.

I grabbed her arm. "Wait! They have guns in there."

"Won't be any fucking good to them if we surprise 'em." With that she gave a hard chop to the door with her right foot. The door popped open like it was running away from a fight. Michelle charged through the open doorway and into the room. "Eat a big one, fascist

70

slime!" she yelled, crossing the small cabin without breaking stride and slamming into the door of the room where I had seen Lily Montevideo less than twenty-four hours before.

That door, like the first one, popped open. Michelle's momentum carried her inside. I was three-quarters of a room behind her.

I heard a man scream. When I got to the smaller room I saw Michelle squared off in a karate stance against a terrified man sitting up in a bed with the covers gathered around him. He was a perfect stranger to me.

"Where is she?" Michelle demanded. It was directed to everyone within the sound of her voice. And that included me.

"I don't know anything!" the man in the bed kept repeating in Spanish.

"Michelle turned to me and jabbed a finger in my chest. "Okay, wise ass, where's Lily?"

I thought for a moment about my life up to the last twenty-four hours. Simple. Uncomplicated. Pleasant even. That's how I would've described it. The most difficult thing facing me up to the day before was the decision where to go hiking. The Pentlands or Blackford Hill. And my only serious worry was that the BBC would move Rockford or Bilko again. Or drop the shows altogether. Funny how things balance out and life makes you pay a price for being boring.

"I don't know," I said. "They must've moved her. She was here yesterday."

"Yeah, sure. And Princess Di was down on the docks humming sailors."

It was then I noticed that the three of us were not alone. Three or four men in officer-whites plus a man dressed like an American military policeman had filled the small room. They demanded to know what was going on.

71

I tried to explain in my best broken English that what we had on our hands was an old world lovers' quarrel. But nobody was buying. One of the officers present was the diplomatic gent who had introduced me to the cabin and the drug trade in the first place. I think he recognized me, but I wasn't sure. The lot of them weren't at all happy that their privacy had been invaded and their doors kicked in. Once again I tried to finesse the situation. It always seemed to work for Jimmy Joe Meeker.

"Scusi, signori," I said, apologetically. "We are so sorry to disturba your peace." I pointed to Michelle. "Maria. She's a go off her head when she hear," I pointed at the man in the bed, "her man, how you say, fool around with another woman. She's a very strong in the head, Maria. Like her father, Guiseppe. It is the way of the people from our village."

The man who seemed to be in charge tried to interrupt me, but I talked through him like he was a screen door. "I tell her. Maria, don't be so stubborn-headed. Talk to the man. But she's a no listen to me. She's a big temper, this one. We beg your pardon a thousand times and I personally invite you all to be our special guests at the next performance of I Fratelli e Sorelle Schiavone." I pounded my chest and smiled, "That's a us."

It seemed to me that I was making some progress. The officer who promised to send me to nose-heaven the day before said something in Spanish to the military policeman. He nodded and grabbed Michelle by the arm.

"Get your fucking hands off me, asshole!" she shouted, planting an elbow into the pit of his stomach. He doubled over and backed up a couple steps toward a neutral corner. Everyone in the room, including me, looked at each other in stunned silence for what seemed longer than the first half of a very dull football match.

Then I looked at Michelle. My eyes motioned towards the door. Then my mouth said, "Run for it!"

We burst through the doorway, the room, the restricted entry double doors and were taking the stairs in twos and threes before I heard the first shouts for us to halt.

We reached the main deck just as the fratelli and sorrelle were being herded off the promenade deck by uniformed guards and angry passengers, some of whom were waving shuffleboard sticks in a threatening manner.

Michelle and I joined them and started up a loud chorus of "Here we go, here we go". We whistled, shouted, banged our drums and gave Italian hand gestures to our pursuers and we then bounded down the ramp to the safety of the dock. We were half-way to the nearest bus stop before I realized Pete Swallow was nowhere to be found.

CHAPTER THIRTEEN

Michelle chewed me out from the moment we got on the bus to Aunt Gina's, where I got off. She slagged me for leading her on a wild-goose chase, for not finding Lily and for forcing her to wear that outrageous costume. She called me names I had never heard before.

Her relentless harangue made it difficult to concentrate on the latest development in the Montevideo case. Like where the hell was she? Was she in danger? Was she even alive? It was impossible to figure out. Impossible for me at least.

Before I got off the bus, I removed the large rubber nose I had been wearing and dropped it in Michelle's lap. "Here," I said. "I'm sure you can find a use for this."

"Fuck you, scumbag!" she shouted at me. Even the bus driver turned around. She picked up the nose and threw it at me. It bounced off a nearby window and landed in an elderly lady's lap, which caused her to shriek.

The bus rolled to a stop and I exited. I could still hear Michelle piling it on through the closed doors.

I walked to the cafe a half-block away. It was mid-afternoon. The lunch crowd had come and gone and the place was nearly empty. The moment I walked through the door I caught Aunt Gina's eye. She did a double take right out of the movies. She cocked her head to one side and squinted through her eyes like she was trying to identify a ship on the horizon.

"Rocco?" she said. "Rocco, is that you in there?"

"Hi, Aunt Gina."

She laughed. It started out slowly, from somewhere in the back of her throat and spread down to her lungs and stomach. It turned into a guffaw and she was holding her sides as if she were experiencing an attack of appendicitis.

Uncle Tony, hearing the convulsive sounds came bursting through the kitchen door. "Gina!" he shouted. "What's the matter? You okay?"

Aunt Gina was bent over with laughter. She pointed at me. "Look who's here," she said, gasping for breath. "It's signor Pantalone." That reopened the sluice-gates to her funny bone. Tony joined in when he realized who it was.

"Rocco," he said, straightening up, "what are you dressed like that for? You in the Festival or something?"

"It's a very long story, Uncle Tony."

Aunt Gina was giggling controllably. "Tony," she said, "run, get the camera. I want a picture of this." Tony disappeared back into the kitchen. Gina took my face in her hands. "I think you look cute, Rocco. You having a good time, son. Being a clown, I mean."

"Aunt Gina, I just stopped by to get rid of these duds. Does Rudy have any clothes upstairs?"

"Clothes? Ha! Clothes, furniture, books, dishes. Everything but himself. That's what he thinks of his mother. A rubbish collector."

"Aunt Gina. He said he would call today. I saw him last night."

"Sure, sure. And the pope is converting to the Church of Scotland."

"No, really. He's been under a lot of pressure at Bilston. The management is harassing the men. Rudy is a shop-steward. He's got a lot to do."

"Twenty-four hours a day he is a shop-steward?"

"Aunt Gina! The clothes."

"Sure, go ahead. Take what you want. Rudy won't miss them. Ha! He would have to come by once in awhile to miss them, wouldn't he?"

Uncle Tony came back through the kitchen door puffing for breath. "I've got the camera, Gina," he said.

For the next five minutes I posed for pictures. First, with Aunt Gina, then with Uncle Tony and finally with both Gina and Tony. Gina persuaded the cafe's solitary customer to snap the picture. Twice. Aunt Gina wanted to send one to my folks. It was no use trying to talk her out of it. Finally, I was allowed to go upstairs for my change of clothes.

I couldn't get out of the cafe, however, without first having a bowl of minestrone and some bread. I also had to promise Aunt Gina once again that I wasn't mixed up in any "funny business", as she put it, and that I would come to dinner within the next five days. I told her to pick a day and I would be there.

She wrapped a couple of Italian doughnuts in a paper napkin and put them in a small paper sack. "You take these with you to that cafe you go to, Rocco," she said, handing me the sack. "Eat them instead of the shortbread. They're better for you." We both smiled. I said goodbye and left the cafe. I felt like a normal person again.

CHAPTER FOURTEEN

It was almost 2 pm. I climbed aboard a number 23 bus near the Royal Scottish Academy and rode it up over the Mound and down George IV Bridge to the University area. I got off near the Royal Infirmary and went in for the news about Morag. And hopefully a visit.

The doctor told me Morag was "one lucky lassie". She had come through the tests without showing any signs of permanent brain damage. In fact, he said, she could be released shortly. Maybe tomorrow.

I walked up to her room on the next floor. I knocked gently on her door and went in without waiting for a reply. She was sitting up in bed watching telly.

"Rocco, darlin'!" she said, smiling as I came into the room.

I walked over to her bed and took her hand. "How are you feeling, Morag?", I said, bending down to plant a little kiss on her bandaged forehead.

"Thank God Glaswegians have hard heads," she laughed. "If I'd have been from your bloody Edinburgh, I'd be right dead by now."

I laughed. "Yeah. We were worried about you, hen. Did Annie call?"

"Aye. She came through about an hour ago. She brought these flowers." Morag pointed to a large bouquet in a vase resting on the little table below the window.

I felt guilty. I should have been the one who brought

the flowers. "I brought you some Italian doughnuts," I said, holding out the bag in front of me.

"Thanks, darlin'," Morag said, smiling. "You eat them. I'm not very hungry just now."

"I'm really sorry about what happened."

"Ach, forget it. It wasn't your fault."

I pulled up the metal chair at the foot of her bed next to her and sat down. I spent the next fifteen minutes explaining to her that it was my fault. At least partially. Then I brought her up to date on the case. The narcotics connection betweeen the *Patagonian Princess* and Calton Hill, the strange appearance and re-disappearance of Lily Montevideo, my encounter with Pete Swallow and Michelle and the tale of the missing script. Morag was flabbergasted. None of it seemed to make any sense to her. With some qualifications, that made two of us. I had hoped she could help me put some of the fragments together.

"Couple of things, Morag," I said, sounding like a detective. "First, did Perez and Montevideo have a good marriage?"

"Good marriage?" she said with a mild start. "What does that have to do with anything?"

"Dunno. Just fishing."

Morag told me that the couple had a very loving, open relationship as far as she knew. The key word there was "open". Morag praised them both for their maturity and understanding. Sounded to me like a lot of fooling around going on, but then I'm old-fashioned.

"Who's this Michelle character?" I asked. "You didn't mention her before."

Morag laughed. "Michelle is a person most people try to forget." That much I already knew. "Have you met her?" I nodded. "Well, then, you know. She's a big, foul-mouthed dyke who dislikes all men and most women."

"What's her connection with Perez and Montevideo?"

"She's a failed actress. She washed out of Rodrigo's acting school several years ago. And she just hung around after that. I mean who could tell Michelle to leave? I guess Rodrigo felt sorry for her and hired her to do odd jobs for the company. Then she became a bloody karate expert and Bob's your uncle — she's a security specialist. Just a glorified bouncer if you ask me. Ach, maybe I'm being too hard on her. She never gave me any trouble. And she worshipped Lily. A more loyal person you couldn't find. Maybe underneath that vulgar exterior is a nice person, but I wouldn't really know anything about that."

"How about Michelle and Swallow. Do they get along?"

"You know, that's the funny part. Two of the most difficult people you'll ever want to meet. Nobody in the company could really get along with either of them when we were at the Royal Court. At least not the actors. But they got on very well. They seemed to understand each other. Know what I mean? It sounds bizarre, given their very different personalities. But maybe not. You know the old saying about opposites attracting each other."

"Yeah. I guess they have their own logic. You said you knew Swallow, didn't you?"

"Aye. Too bloody well, I'm afraid."

"That's what I thought you said. But when I mentioned your name he didn't know it."

"I'm not surprised. He's such a wanker. Those he considers to be beneath him might as well be trilobites or something. He treats actors like shite."

I smiled. "Nice, you lot in the theatre."

"It's really not as bad as all that, Rocco. I mean Rodrigo was a genius. A political and creative genius. People worshipped the ground he walked on. He could have started his own religion if he'd wanted to. Folk were that devoted to him. But talk about attracting opposites. Poor Rodrigo. He had more than his share of opposites around him. A lot of bitches and wankers as far as I'm concerned." She turned her head away from me. I could see fresh tears spilling onto her cheeks.

She was getting tired. I stood up and kissed her on the forehead. I held out the bag of Aunt Gina's doughnuts and insisted she take one. She reluctantly obliged. I told her I had places to go and would look in on her later. I didn't tell her one of the places I had to go was .the George Hotel. I wanted to find out what had happened to the "wanker" named Pete Swallow.

CHAPTER FIFTEEN

It was mid-afternoon by the time I reached the George. The 3.30 performances were just getting underway. Fiasco Job Job, two comics who were presenting "the positive side of nihilism", were just about to do their stuff at the Celtic Lodge. I had ticked them off in the programme since I first saw them in London at the Tricycle in Kilburn doing a miners' benefit. And an American play about radicals from the '60s facing up to the Reagan '80s was raising its curtain at a venue in the Grass-market. Maybe tomorrow, I thought.

I walked up the stairs to Pete Swallow's suite. Michelle opened the door on the third knock. "What do you want?" she said. Raw sewage would have received a warmer welcome.

"Has Pete turned up yet?" I asked

Michelle laughed and turned her head back into the room. "Hey, Pete. Sherlock Holmes wants to know if you've turned up yet."

"Who is it, Michelle?" The voice came from inside the room and belonged to Pete Swallow.

"It's that comedian from California. Rocky Raccoon." She laughed and slapped her own knee.

"Gi's a break, Michelle," I said, extending the pipe of peace.

She stopped laughing. "In your hat, asshole. You made a damn fool outta me. Twice. There ain't gonna be no third time. Ya dig?"

"I may be way off base here, but I detect a note of hostility between us."

"You bet your sweet ass there is. I'm tired of looking at your ugly face, so why don't you be a good little boy and shove off."

"Michelle!" shouted an irritated Swallow. "What on earth are you doing? Invite the man to step inside."

Michelle sneered at me and then stepped aside slowly like a boulder rolling from the entrance to a crypt. Crypt might have been the right word. Like in the old story in the Bible that Christians like to bring up every year around the time of the spring equinox. For when Michelle rolled away from the doorway and I stepped into the room I saw, sitting politely in a chair across from Pete Swallow, the resurrection of Lily Montevideo. She smiled very slightly as I approached her.

Swallow stood up and stepped between us. "May I present . . ." he started to say.

"No, let me guess," I said, interrupting him. "You're Lily Montevideo. Formerely of Calton Hill and the *Patagonian Princess*. Am I right?"

Lily Montevidoe extended her right hand without standing up. It was cool and damp.

"Quite a surprise, this, eh?" said Swallow, gesturing toward Lily Montevideo with his eyes. "Freed from the clutches of the desperadoes and now sitting here larger than life itself. Who would have thought it possible?"

"Yeah. Dodgy chap, life," I said, suppressing my anger.

"I beg your pardon," Swallow said, as if he hadn't heard me.

"I said life's funny, ain't it? I mean we all thought Ms Montevideo might have been kidnapped and her life in danger. I even dressed up like a refugee from a medieval circus and set out to rescue her with a geezer who disappeared in the middle of what proved to be a very hairy situation." I looked at Michelle who was standing at parade-rest behind the widow. "Then I get ragged for failing to rescue said kidnappee on a public bus by a karate expert who's got a chemical waste dump for a mouth. Now, what I want to know is what the hell is going on here? Could someone let me in on the gag."

"Gag?" said Swallow as if the word had been kicked out of the Oxford English Dictionary for being too American. Or too stupid. Or both.

"Yeah. Gag. Joke. Rib. Tickle. Con. Scam. I think you get the picture."

Swallow giggled sarcastically. "There is no 'gag', as you say. I'm not sure I like your tone, old fellow."

"Then that makes two of us. Old fellow."

"I think you have got the wrong impression. You see, Ms Montevideo thankfully escaped those criminals on the boat. On her own, actually. In fact, she made her escape only moments before we boarded it. She spotted me on the promenade deck where you had instructed us to go. With the confusion we created I was able to make contact and spirit her off the boat and back to the hotel without being intercepted. It was a bit of rather good luck, wouldn't you say?"

"Yeah, rather." I looked around the room. Everyone was smiling politely. Even Michelle. I reached into my pocket for a smoke and my matches. "Type it up," I

81

said, once I got the cigarette going, "and I'll read it my little nephew before he goes to bed at night."

"Your nephew?"

"Yeah. He's mad about fairy-tales." The smile drained from Swallow's face like cheap motor oil from an old car.

Michelle slammed her fist into her hand. "Let me pop him!" she said. "Just one time. That's all."

Swallow held up his hand. "Michelle! Please."

"Look," I said. "I don't want to be the one to come between you two, but I'm not leaving here until I get some straight answers." Michelle made snorting noises through her nose. "And you can tell Godzilla I'm through being pushed around."

" I really don't see your point, old man," said Swallow. "I told you how it happened. That should be enough." The long, uncomfortable silence that followed told both of us that it wasn't.

Lily Montevideo stood up and motioned me to the chair beside her. "Please, my friend. Won't you sit down?"

Swallow turned to her. "No, Lily," he said, shaking his head. "He doesn't need to know anything more. He's not on the pay-roll. We don't owe him a bloody thing. Money, explanations, nothing." Swallow shot me a glance that two hours ago I might have thought impossible.

Lily Montevideo walked between us. "It's alright, Peter," she said, reassuringly. "I *want* to give him an explanation." She sat down in the mohair chair. She looked at me and smiled weakly. Her eyes were the kind of blue they used in Dresden when they made all those porcelain cups and dishes. Blue and sad.

She cleared her throat before speaking. "I understand from Peter and Michelle that today's effort to rescue me was your idea." I nodded tentatively, not knowing

82

whether to take a bow or make an excuse. "I thank you for your attempt. It was ingenious. Have you ever considered a career in the theatre?"

"Not since I forgot my lines in the sixth-grade Christmas pageant at school."

Lily Montevideo chuckled noticeably. "Michelle said you struck quite a pose as signore Pantalone."

I raised my eyebrows and looked in Michelle's direction. "I said he looked like a fucking turd," she snapped, turning away and walking to another part of the room.

I shook my head. "She has a remarkable way with words, doesn't she?"

"Michelle is a very trusted friend, senor," said Lily Montevideo. The temperature in the room plunged ten degrees. There was a brief silence during which I was the one made to feel out of line. Me!

Lily Montevideo cleared her throat and looked at Pete Swallow. "Given the circumstances," she said, "I feel you are entitled to an explanation concerning my presence on the *Patagonian Princess*."

"So do I."

"Essentially, what Peter has told you is correct. I was taken to the ship last night by the people who attacked Rodrigo." When her voice came to the name of her dead husband it began to quiver noticeably.

"I was injected with a narcotic," she continued, "which caused me to lose consciousness. When I awoke I found myself aboard the ship. I had been awake only a short time when you appeared at the cabin door. The narcotic had not completely worn off. I was still quite groggy."

"Who was the pistolero with you? He tried to sell me a ton of cocaine."

"He is a colonel in the Chilean secret police."

"DINA?"

"Yes. Colonel Vega is his name. Our paths have

83

crossed before. He wanted me to produce a copy of the script to Rodrigo's new play."

"Did you?"

"Senor. I have been tortured before. In Chile. I told you I had crossed paths with Vega before. They would have to kill me first. I think Vega knows that. Besides, to be honest, I don't know where the script is."

"But Swallow here . . ." I said, pointing to the man in question.

"It does not matter what anyone says. Rodrigo did not tell me the location of the script. I only know that it is supposed to contain the names of several British government officials, military personnel as well, whose careers would be put at serious risk should their names and deeds become public."

"And you really don't know where the script is?"

"Senor! If I told DINA under the threat of torture that I didn't, you can believe that I don't."

"Sorry. I didn't mean to imply . . ."

"Please. There is no need for an apology." Lily Montevideo rose from her chair. Her hands were clasped together at her waist. "Now, if you will excuse me, I have a show to attend to," her eyes left the room and her voice started to unravel, "and a husband to bury." She nodded her head towards me, turned and quietly left the room.

Swallow stood up and started walking to the front door. The indication was that I should follow. I stood up and followed. "So, where does that leave us?" I said to his back.

He turned. "It leaves us nowhere," he said. "The matter is now totally in the hands of the authorities. I hope you have the good sense to go home, put the kettle on and have a nice cup of tea."

"In other words, I can take that trip to Skye, right?"

"I beg your pardon."

"You want I should take a powder and drop out of sight."

Swallow grinned. "Nothing personal, old fellow, but yes, something like that." He reached into his pocket and produced two fifty pound notes. "Here," he said, "Lily wants you to have this." He tucked the bills into my shirt pocket. "For your trouble."

I patted my shirt pocket. "Ah. The buy off."

Swallow shook his head. "No, nothing like that. Lily is a very generous person and wishes to show you her appreciation. It's the right thing to do. Believe me." Swallow put his hand on my shoulder and opened the door. "Goodbye, Conigliaro."

"Adios, shithead!" Michelle said, from the back of the room.

The door shut in my face before I could say anything. Before I could go into a routine where I would tell Swallow I wasn't the kind of guy who could be bought and throw the money in his face. But it didn't matter. I wouldn't have done it anyway. I *am* the kind of guy who can be bought. Everyone is. But one hundred pounds isn't even an acceptable deposit. I should've thrown the dough in his face because the price was puny and insulting. But I wouldn't have done that, either. I always need all the readies I can lay my hands on, regardless of the source. Oh, what has become of principles and stuff like that?

CHAPTER SIXTEEN

So, in a manner of speaking, I was all dressed up with no place to go. Let's see. There was no longer a kidnappee to rescue; no clues to the whereabouts of the missing script; no case to solve anymore; no one needed my professional services; I was told to get lost. Period. I had a hundred fresh pounds burning a hole in my pocket that I hadn't had the day before. Pretty good, right? Cleared the decks for some serious Fringe.

I stopped by the Fruitmarket Gallery Cafe across the street from the City Art Centre for a cappuccino. The coffee there is not quite as good as what Helen makes, but the cups are bigger.

Downstairs from the second floor cafe, in the main gallery, was a curious exhibition by two Russian painters. A lot of dark, satiric canvases, mostly of Stalin. Like Stalin sitting barefoot before a mirror admiring himself; Stalin holding session with the Greek muses and one entitled "The Birth of Socialist Realist Painting", in which the muse of art is tracing a shadow outline of Uncle Joe's puss on the base of a statue. Pretty humorous stuff, really. As was the huge portrait of Ronald Reagan as a centaur.

After my coffee I hiked the Fleshmarket steps to the Fringe Office to pick up another guide. The queue for tickets wound fifty feet out the door and down Old Mercat Close. A couple dozen people were milling around on the sidewalk out front. Most of them were poring intently over their Fringe Guides and Daily Diaries like they were tip sheets for the races at Ayr. Others were passing out leaflets to anyone who would take them.

I quickly thumbed through the ninety-page guide. I ticked off Mark Miwurdz and the political cabaret for the third time. This time there would be nothing preventing me from making it. One of the leaflets that found its way into my hand as I walked the gauntlet in front of the Fringe Office announced that Roland Muldoon would be appearing at the political cabaret with his one-man stand-up comedy act.

That clinched it. Ever since I saw him do his

86

"Full Confessions of a Socialist" at the People's Theatre Coalition in Frisco some years ago, I've been a fan. I saw one of his productions in London before I came up to Edinburgh. The Left-Wing Teds, a socialist 'teddy boy' rock group, and Claire Muldoon, who did a chillingly accurate imitation of Margaret Thatcher had joined him. The leaflet said they were going to appear in the cabaret as well. This cabaret was certainly shaping up as something not to be missed.

Loudon Wainright and Hank Wangford were appearing at the Fringe Club. So was the finals of the busking competition. There was also a special late-night show being put on by Amandala, the theatre company of the black South African ANC, at the Assembly Rooms, and Anthony Zerbe was back with his E. E. Cummings show. I saw him last year. One of the best shows of the Fringe. Looked like a good night.

I called Annie to interest her in an evening at the Fringe. She was reluctant at first. The SWP was having a disco at Annabell's.

"Come on, hen," I pleaded. "I'm springing for the whole shootin' match. Theatre, cabaret, drinks. The works."

"What about the tea?" She drove a hard bargain.

"Got time for a Wimpy's or a salad at Henderson's, but that's about all. It's 6.15 now and the show starts at 7.30."

"Okay. Shall we not just meet at Henderson's, then?"

"I was figuring on Wimpy's, actually."

"Ach, ya numptie. I'll no' be going to Wimpy's."

"Okay, okay. Henderson's it is. Can you be there in half an hour?"

"I think so. But I want to go through to the hospital, first, and drop off a copy of *Socialist Worker* to Morag."

I laughed. "You people don't give up, do you?"

"What?"

87

"Selling the party press to people with brain concussions. For shame."

"She asked for a copy."

"Sure, sure. Bring a bundle. You can make the rounds of the intensive care ward. It's just the thing to read while you're hooked up to a heart-lung machine." I laughed again. It was a friendly laugh following a friendly joke. However, Annie didn't look at it that way.

"You're dead funny, Rocco. You know that? You Americans. You can just forget about going to my sister's."

"Hey! That's not a nice thing to say."

"You should know."

"Hey, I'm sorry."

"What?"

"It was irresistible. I didn't mean anything by it. You know I look upon Tony Cliff as a father-figure."

"Ach! Stop your yappin'. You're nippin' my heid. Do you want to go out tonight, or what? It's almost half six."

"Okay. See you at Henderson's at seven."

"Right. At Henderson's."

"Ciao, mi amore. Give my regards to Morag."

I hung up the phone and walked out of the booth. The sun was still high over the castle in the west. I hiked up past St. Giles to where the Lawnmarket begins and turned north and began the descent of the Mound. I took the Playfair Steps down to the cement walk that passed betweeen the Royal Scottish Academy and Princes Street Gardens.

Painters and crafts merchants had their products lined up on the black bar-fence that runs from the stairs, over the train tracks out of Waverly almost to Princes Street. I stopped to admire the several watercolour prints of Edinburgh landscapes. It was the third time I'd been by.

I wanted to send one to the folks back home but I was having difficulty deciding which one. I promised myself the next time I passed by I would choose.

Crowds formed circles around three different groups of buskers. Inside one circle three young men were miming the race scene from *Chariots of Fire* while the theme music squawked from a portable cassette tape player. Next door a band was playing. But this wasn't any ordinary band. Their instruments consisted of large pieces of industrial plastic pipes, tubes, ducts and other effluvia to be found on large building sites. I couldn't see what was going on inside the third ring.

Something else caught my eye. Something other than the chalk-artist's drawing on the sidewalk on Princes Street. I had almost walked on a superb five square-foot chalk rendering of the Mona Lisa. I've seen expensive colour pictures of the real thing, the one they keep in Paris, but this one looked just as good. Maybe even better.

What captured my attention was a person sitting on a bench at the top of the Gardens. Rather it was what he was holding between his hands that caught my attention. It was the latest edition of the *Evening News*. Its headline read: ACTRESS ESCAPES — ACCUSES KGB.

My eyes, head and heart nearly ceased functioning all at the same time. The feet, however, kept on walking until they bumped into the fence at Princes Street. The sharp pain experienced in my shins served to kick-start the rest of my vital organs. I walked around the fence to the crossing, but I didn't wait for the little green man to give me the high sign to cross the busiest street in town. I sprinted across the four lanes, beating an oncoming cab by a good step or two. Then I did the same thing across Hanover Street to the newsagent at the corner. I literally ripped a copy of the *News* from his hand. I gave him a fifty-pence piece, but didn't have the patience to wait for my change. I dashed into the doorway of a closed-down shop and began reading the story:

Internationally known actress Lily Montevideo, who disappeared two days ago following the brutal murder of her equally famed husband, actor-playwright Rodrigo Perez, held a press conference this afternoon at the George Hotel.

Ms Montevideo told both the press and the authorities that she was kidnapped from Calton Hill and drugged by agents of the KGB, the state security police of the Soviet Union.

"They murdered Rodrigo and abducted me," she said of the KGB, "because Rodrigo and I are revolutionaries who dared expose the Soviet betrayals of socialism in our work."

Although the Soviet Union has no consular representation in Edinburgh, the Russian Meyerhold Theatre Company is performing two plays by Bertolt Brecht in the International Festival's Usher Hall. It is widely known that agents of the KGB accompany Soviet artists when they tour abroad.

When reached in London, a spokesman for the Soviet Embassy said the charges were "preposterous" and "but another example of anti-Soviet hysteria".

The same spokesman claimed not to have any personal knowledge of Mr Perez or Ms Montevideo. He also said no official statement would be forthcoming from his government unless it was to answer "the lies and slanders against the Soviet people".

In Edinburgh, Chief Inspector William McNab said that the police were checking Ms Montevideo's story. "We will spare no amount of time or manpower," he said, "to get to the bottom of this double crime."

It is widely speculated that MI6 has already been called onto the scene to investigate KGB activities here.

In London, Mr Jeffrey Archer, best-selling author,

former MP, Deputy Chairman of the Tory Party, and confidant to Whitehall Ministers, said he would urge his colleagues in government to seek "retaliatory measures" against the Soviet Union.

Foreign Secretary, Sir Geoffrey Howe, said he was shocked when he heard the charges. If they prove correct, he commented, then "appropriate representations would be made to the Soviet government".

I should have tossed the *News* into the rubbish box at the next corner, shrugged my shoulders, said something like "c'est la vie," and proceeded on to Henderson's to meet Annie. That's what I should have done. I wanted to. But I couldn't. It's one thing to buy me off with pocket money, but it's quite another to play me for a sucker. I don't play the sap for nobody. I mean, that's why Sam Spade sent Brigid O'Shaunessy down, right?

CHAPTER SEVENTEEN

I banged on the door to Swallow's digs until my knuckles turned red. "Open up in there, damn it!" I shouted, loud enough for the whole floor to hear.

A minute or so later I heard Michelle's voice bulldoze it's way through the closed door. "Who the fuck's out there?"

"Humphrey Bogart, sweetheart. Open this goddamn door before I turn it into toothpicks."

"Go away, shithead!"

I began kicking the door. Other doors along the corridor opened and eyes and noses peeped out tentatively to see what the commotion was all about. I didn't care. I kept kicking the door. Then it opened suddenly and a hand reached out and yanked me inside.

"You're becoming a royal pain in the ass," Michelle

91

said, shoving me into the room. "You fucking know that?"

"Where's Lily?" I said

"Wouldn't you like to know?"

"Yeah. Where is she?"

"She's not here."

"Well, then. Nothing personal, Michelle, but I think I'll just take a look around and see for myself." I stepped off in the direction of one of the bedrooms.

Michelle stomped over in front of the door, planting herself like a California redwood. "Your ears need cleanin', buddy? I said she ain't here."

"Look. Somebody's been jerking me around and I don't like it."

"Too bad, cream-puff."

"You were here when Lily told me the Chilean secret police killed Rodrigo and kidnapped her."

"So?"

I took the rolled up copy of the *Evening News* from my back pocket, unrolled it and stuck it in front of her face. "Take a gander at that."

She looked at the paper for a few seconds then knocked it out of my hand.

"What do you make of that?" I asked.

"I don't make nothin' outta nothin'. If that's what Lily said, then that's good enough for me.

"But this afternoon . . ."

"Fuck this afternoon! Maybe she was feeding you a bowl of rice krispies just to get you out of her hair. Man, you're like a case of the crabs that won't go away."

"Look, Michelle, lighten up, will you? Hey! I'm one of the good guys."

"My ass!"

"Something's going on here that doesn't make sense. Lily can clear it up. Maybe she's still in trouble."

"The only one in trouble is you. Now, you better

92

scram if you know what's good for you." She started toward me.

"Michelle! You know I'm right."

"I only know what Pete says. Come on, time to hit the road." She grabbed my arm and began pushing me toward the door.

"What does Pete say?"

"He thinks maybe you're an agent."

"An agent? Are you joking?"

"That's what he says. I believe him. Lily does, too."

"Be serious. Who'd hire me to be an agent?"

"I know. That's what I said. But somebody drops out of the sky like you did and offers to help like you did. Well, it sorta makes a body suspicious." Michelle reached for the doorknob. I grabbed her hand. She didn't care for that. "Take your hand offa me, you fucking pervert!" I released my grip.

"Look. A friend of mine, a person who knew Rodrigo asked me to do something. I wish I had told her to go to hell, but I didn't."

Michelle squinted through her eyes. "Yeah? Who was this friend? One of Rodrigo's little playmates?"

"Just a friend. Really."

"Look, Conigliaro, a lot of nasty shit has been goin' down and we can't afford to trust nobody. You dig?"

"Yeah, I know. Things are tough all over." Michelle smirked and nodded her head. "Where is she, Michelle?"

"Holy fucking Christ in a pantsuit! You're something else, man. What is it going to take for you to get it through your head that we don't want your ass around here?" She clenched her fist and waved it in my face. "You paid up your dental insurance, fool?"

Michelle took a large step away from me. She reared back her right, black-booted, steel-toed leg. She let fly.

"Shit!" she shouted, as her foot landed full force into the wall a good two feet away from me. I uncrouched and looked up at her. She looked at me for an instant then turned away. "She's at the Assembly Rooms," she said softly.

"Did you say Assembly Rooms?"

"Yeah. The fucking Assembly Rooms! Are you deaf? She and Pete went over about an hour ago to work out something with the management about the show."

"Thanks," I said. I opened the door and left without saying another word. I didn't want to give her time to develop second thoughts about revealing Lily Montevideo's whereabouts to me.

It only took a few minutes to get to the Assembly Rooms. But it took twice that long to get through the queues that had jammed the entrance. One queue, I learned, was to see Pookiesnackenburger. Another was waiting to see a spectacle performed by a group from Poland everybody was raving about. It was called *The End of Europe*. A subject Poles should know something about. A third was the queue for the political cabaret.

I politely slogged my way through the jam and up the stairs to the administrative offices. I was told by a very thin woman sitting behind a desk that Lily and Pete left a half hour ago. I told her I was with the company so I was able to get a second-hand story about the meeting they had with the management.

Seems the Assembly Rooms stood to lose a lot of sterling if the show was totally cancelled. And if it was, someone would have to pay. Simple as that. Someone always has to pay. It's the wages of life. What makes it interesting — life, that is — is trying to make sure it's the other guy that gets stuck with the tab.

The woman behind the desk let me use her phone to call the George Hotel. Michelle answered. She said Lily and Pete hadn't returned. She sounded worried, but with Michelle, who could tell?

I walked back down to the lobby. With maybe two to

three hundred people packed in there like immigrants waiting to be processed at Ellis Island, my eyes had to meet Annie's. She was near the door and working her way inside. Her neck was rotating like a ventriloquist's dummy, like she was desperately looking for someone. Me. A strange look of recognition swept across her face when she saw me.

Another moment earlier and I could have ducked into the toilet and waited until she left. Until she cooled down. She wasn't looking exactly chuffed. But I was trapped and made my way through the throng toward her. I tried to smile, but I had a feeling that it came out all wrong. Before I could say, "I can explain everything," she said, "I'm sorry I'm late."

"Say what?"

"I got hung up at hospital with Morag. We got to talking. Ach, you know how Morag is. I came straight over here."

I looked forlornly at my watch. Well, it's too late now. The show was sold out anyway by the time I got here."

"I really am sorry. Did you have your tea at Henderson's?"

"No."

"Well, let's go, then. Maybe we can take in a late show somewhere."

I pretended to sulk a bit. "Okay. I guess it's all we can do."

"I'll treat."

"Oh, alright."

I talked her into going to La Lanterna across the street from Henderson's. They serve a tagliatelle in tomato and cream sauce that never fails to bring tears of joy to my eyes. It wasn't hard talking Annie out of Henderson's.

She knew my dislike for the wholewheat nationalism that characterizes the place. Besides, it reminds me of too many places in San Francisco.

95

We took a table near the rear of the restaurant. Annie had her bundle of *Socialist Workers* with her. She handed me one and insisted I read Eamon McCann's article about American television. Like now. I rolled my eyes and turned to the article. I was half-way through when my eyes jumped the column to an article that was much more interesting to me. It was an obituary of Rodrigo Perez. The article was a critical, but generous, tribute to his work. The writer went into the story of the battle between Perez and the Home Office over *Ships in the Night* and offered the speculation that MI6 had assassinated him.

It went on to say some other things that I already knew, but the last third of the article contained two bits that I didn't know. The first was that Perez was attacked and beaten up two years ago in the suburbs of Paris by "thugs, either members of, or in the employ of the Stalinist French Communist Party".

The second thing I didn't know was that Kate Wallace, the missing performer who left the cast, was originally from Edinburgh. The first bit of news added to the confusion generated by Lily Montevideo's accusations in the press. The info about Kate Wallace was a real surprise. Why didn't Swallow tell me that she was from Edinburgh? Why didn't he try to contact her through friends or relatives in the area? Why had he assumed that she returned to her flat in London?

I heard the distant sound of a voice calling my name. "This is earth calling Rocco. Come in Rocco." It was Annie.

"What? Huh? Oh." I smiled.

"I've never known Eamon McCann to have such an effect on you. I thought you didn't fancy his writing."

I thrust the paper in Annie's face. "Did you see this?" I said, pointing to the article on Perez.

"Aye. But I haven't read it yet. Why?"

"Who is Ian Robertson?" I asked, reading the name of the article's author.

"A bloke in the SWP. He's a teacher. He stays in Stockbridge."

"You mean he lives here in Edinburgh?"

"Aye. What are you getting so worked up about?"

"There were some things in the article . . ."

"I thought you were finished with that business."

"Yeah, so did I. Do you have this guy's phone number?"

"Yes."

"Give it to me."

"It's at home."

"Let's go get it. I want to talk to him."

"Okay."

"Now."

"Not now, ya daftie. I want my tea, first. Look, here it comes now."

The waitress slid the tagliatelle under my nose and sprinkled cheese on it. The noodles, not my nose. The aroma almost put me into a trance. I buttered a roll, took a generous swallow of wine and dived into my pasta. For the next thirty minutes I said nothing. I savoured my food and thought about Kate Wallace. Every now and then I heard voices. Annie's voice. I guess she was speaking to me and I guess I answered. I really couldn't say.

CHAPTER EIGHTEEN

I looked up Ian Robertson's number in the telephone directory and phoned him from a call box just outside the restaurant. He wasn't in. There was still light in the sky. In fact, it was just before twilight. I suggested to Annie that we take a run someplace in her car. I suggested Blackford Hill. I could phone Ian Robertson again in an hour or so.

Each of Edinburgh's seven hills has views more interesting than the next. Blackford Hill is in the southern part of the city off Morningside Road. The new observatory is up there. Outside of the Pentlands it must have the largest hiking area in Edinburgh and its environs.

We hiked all the way around the hill, ending on the western slope overlooking a small duck pond. The Morningside area lay beyond it and the castle and central Edinburgh beyond that to the north. We spoke very little until we found a place to sit.

There we watched the blue of the night wash over the sky. It was like watching a giant set of trains in someone's basement. Everything was in miniature. The pond, the houses, the trees. You could almost imagine that somewhere someone was throwing switches and turning knobs to make it all happen. Each moment a darker shade of sky descended it seemed like hundreds of artificial lights twinkled on. Like the geezer at the switchboard had it all computerized.

I reached for Annie's hand. It was soft and warm and reassuring. We talked about the sites down below. Annie said the duck pond reminded her of the pond at the Buttes Chaumont in Paris. I wanted to know the names of the churches whose spires poked through the sky. She said she didn't know and didn't much care. I tried to compare Edinburgh with San Francisco, but it didn't mean much to her since she'd never been there.

"What are we going to do when this business is all over?" I said, shifting gears.

"What?" she said. Annie says "what?" a lot. She's told me she's not sure if it's my accent or she is losing her hearing. I say "what?" a lot, too. It's definitely our accents. And vocabularies.

"I mean, when this case, such as it is, is behind us. What are we going to do?"

"Do about what?"

"About each other."

"What about each other?"

"I mean, you know, our future. Like do we have one together, or what? Do you ever think about it?"

"Yes, of course."

"Well, what do you think?"

"I don't know. It's so difficult to think about the future. I thought you'd be back in America by now."

"Well, as you can see, I'm not."

"Don't you get homesick, sometimes?"

"Sure. Sort of. But it's something I can live with. What I want to know is if you're someone I can live with."

"You can always stay at my place. You know that."

"I'm not talking about 'staying with', I'm talking about 'living with'."

"What?"

"Staying with. Living with. They have two different meanings."

"They mean the same in Scotland."

"Yeah, I know. But how do you mean it?"

"Hmm?"

I took out a cigarette and lit it. It was a signal to Annie that I was dropping the subject. She was only too pleased to oblige. It wasn't that she didn't take me seriously. Or our relationship. It was just that it was really difficult to get her to open up and talk about it. At first I thought maybe she was an emotional basket case. Then I thought maybe I was. And then later I thought we both were. Now, I don't know. I think it's cultural differences more than anything else.

There is something about folk from northern Protestant countries. They can be as guarded as the Berlin Wall when it comes to emotional matters. "British reserve" only hints at it. In Scotland, the religion was and is Calvinism. And that, in some ways, makes the English to the south appear as warm and expressive as the French or Italians.

I'm no California human-growth-potential nut who wears his emotions around the neck like a lobster bib for all to see, but I'm different from Annie. From the Scottish. At times, it seems to me Hadrian's Wall did more than separate the Romans from the Picts. Sometimes these cultural "no-go" zones really get up my nose. At other times, I just accept it the best way I can. This was one of those other times. Low-level frustration. Besides, I had other things on my mind. Both Annie and I knew that. I put my arm around her, kissed her on the mouth and told her I wanted to get to a phone.

CHAPTER NINETEEN

I phoned Ian Robertson when we got back to Annie's. This time he was in. He told me he went to school with Kate. He also said he hadn't seen her for years and really didn't know where she could be found. Back when he knew her she had lived with her mother at Muirhouse, one of the big public housing schemes in Edinburgh. But, he warned, that was nearly fifteen years ago.

I thanked him for his help and began flipping through the pages of the phone directory almost before I had put the receiver down. He said he thought Kate's mother's name was Margaret. There were three columns of Wallaces in the directory, but only a handful of Margarets and "M"s. Annie knew the location of the prefix numbers and that narrowed it down even more,

There were only two Muirhouse Wallaces that were listed under M. If Kate's mother still lived there and hadn't remarried, I knew where to find her. Why aren't more things in life as simple as that?

I went to bed feeling that maybe I was about to get a handle on this case. It would be about time.

It was raining when I stepped outside the next morning. It rains a lot in Edinburgh. It's like Seattle and Portland. I like the rain as much as the next person. Actually, more. And it is one of the few things about Frisco that I miss. But I don't like rain every day. Or even every other day. Especially not during the Festival. Besides, I only have one pair of shoes and they have gum soles that like to hydroplane on the hilly sidewalks of the city centre during rainy spells. Makes fleeing the bad guys in wet weather a dodgy proposition.

The sky was grey. Greyer than the grey buildings. Heavier, too. As I walked to the bus stop the rain eased off, becoming a slight little spit in the face. Drizzle isn't the right word to describe it. Too negative. I guess spit isn't any better. It was more like tiny champagne bubbles popping all over my face and hands. It tickled. It was the kind of rain in which, if you were a writer, you could take a long walk down a solitary country lane pondering heavy-duty creative thoughts. If you were just an average punter it might help clear your head so you could better face some of life's nagging little problems. Like how are you going to face another day on the dole. Or, for that matter, in your job. Me, I thought about Kate Wallace and what, if anything, she had to do with the murder of Rodrigo Perez.

Muirhouse is one of Edinburgh's largest council estates. It's on the west side of town, away from the castle, the Caledonian Hotel, Usher Hall, museums, and other places where the well-bred and the tourists like to go.

Edinburgh is ringed by large housing schemes that

101

stand like a ragged peasant army guarding the king and his retainers. Wester Hailes, Craigmillar, Bingham, Pilton, Muirhouse. Concrete blocks with windows. Those that aren't boarded up. Monuments to a society that dumps its post-industrial products into human battery farms. Although, here the process has been reversed. No force-feeding to fatten the livestock to insure maximum profit. The profit has already been made. Instead of being prepared for the slaughter, they have been mothballed to oblivion.

I got off the bus and walked onto the estate. Large rectangular blocks, some with aluminium-fronted balconies that made them more like rubbish skips, and dozens of three and four storey buildings constructed from some dark-stained, pebbled substance. In the middle, if there is a middle to such a sprawl, stood a twenty-storey high-rise block with sharp edges that make it look like a filing cabinet for a two hundred-foot office secretary. All examples from the Frank Lloyd Wrong School of Architecture. If they were people instead of buildings, they would be hanging around street corners smoking cigarettes and looking to pick fights with strangers.

Five thousand people must live in Muirhouse. Maybe more. Decent folk. Those who haven't been turned into dross and lumpenized. A hundred feet in the air some of them. Living behind damp walls, leaking balconies and falling tiles. It was reported in the papers that millions were needed to repair these crumbling chateaux. As I climbed the stairs to one of the blocks I wondered if there would be Muirhouses under socialism. Then I thought about the endless ocean of dreary concrete housing estates in Eastern Europe and the Soviet Union.

I found the door to the fourth-floor flat of one of the two Muirhouse M. Wallaces. I knocked and waited, but no one answered. I knocked again and tried not to look like I could even remotely be mistaken for a DHSS spy.

I may not have been in Britain very long, but I have seen *Boys from the Black Stuff*. Still, no one answered. I tried not to take it personally.

I walked back down the stairs and on to the building where the other M. Wallace lived. I knocked on the door. I could hear movement inside the flat. A moment later the door opened. A woman of about sixty, large, with grey curly hair and a slightly reddish colour to her cheeks stood before me.

"Mrs Wallace?" I asked.

"Aye, that's right," she said. "And who might you be?"

"Mrs Wallace. Do you have a daughter named Kate?"

"Yer no' fae the polis, are ya, son?"

I smiled. "No, no. It's nothing like that."

"American, aren't ya, son?"

"Yes. That's right."

"Well, then. I didnae think you were from the polis. You're no' from the bloody CIA, are ya?"

I laughed out loud. "Not hardly."

"A friend of Kate's, did ya say?"

"Well, not exactly. A friend of a friend."

Mrs Wallace extended her hand past me. "Well, you better come in out the smirr." I stepped inside. "Ach, it's a dreichin' mornin'. You'll be steppin' ben the hoose for a cuppa tea?"

"Thank you." I followed Mrs Wallace into the little sitting-room, where she told me to sit down. She went into the kitchen to put the kettle on. A moment later she returned with a plate of chocolate biscuits, shortbread and jam cakes.

"I'll bring the tea through in a minute," she said. "Mind you, it's no' very fancy. Just plain, boring black tea."

"That'll be fine, Mrs Wallace."

"Oh, aye. Now son, help yoursel' to some biscuits."

She pushed the plate towards me and returned to the kitchen. I had a shortbread. She came back with a teapot and two cups on a small metal tray. She set it down on the table and poured the tea into the cups.

"Do ya take a wee bit a milk and sugar?"

"A little of both, yes. Thank you." Mrs Wallace set the cup in front of me and poured some milk from a pint carton into a cup. She followed with a teaspoon of sugar.

"There ya go." She sat down and poured herself a cup. "Me, I take mine wi' only a wee drop a milk. Now, son, ya say you're no' the polis. I ken that a'right. Ya dinnae stay in the Gorbals for thirty years wi'out ya ken who the polis is at first sight."

"You're from Glasgow, then," I said. I read somewhere that in its day the Gorbals was to Glasgow what Harlem is to New York.

"Oh, aye. Ya didny think I was fae Edinburgh, dee ya?"

"Sorry."

"Oh, it isnae a bad place. Just a wee bit unfriendly. Ya can go doon tae the shops on Princes Street or oot tae git your messages and speak tae naebody. It isnae friendly, that. When I first came through after the old yin died it nearly made me demented. Ya know? Havin' naebody tae blether wi'. I was dead skunnered at first. But I had my sister and the weans, so I got used tae it. Have ya no' been through tae Glasgow, son?"

"Aye. I mean, yes."

"Well, then ya know what I'm on aboot. This is a fine wee town, a'right. But some of the folk. They cannae be bothered tae gi' ya the time a day. Sarky bastards. Fur coat an' nae knickers. Ya know?"

It must have been the puzzled look on my face because Mrs Wallace abruptly shifted the conversation. "Ach, ya didny come all the way from America tae listen tae an old woman girn an' greet at ya, dee ya? Ya said ya wanted tae talk wi' my Kate."

"That's right. Do you know where I can find her?"

"Ya ken she disny live wi' her auld mam. She's got a wee flat doon in London."

"Yes, I know. But she's up here for the Festival. Surely you must know that."

"Don't get struppy wi' me, son. It'll dee your cause nae good. I'm tellin' ya."

"I'm sorry, Mrs Wallace. It's just that Kate left the show and I'd like to find her."

"What for?"

"Just to ask her a few questions, that all."

"Who dee ya say ya was workin' for?"

"I'm not working for anybody. I have a friend. My flat mate, actually. Morag Blair. She's a friend of Kate's. I think they worked together in the theatre. Morag's quite upset about Rodrigo Perez's murder. The playwright. Did you hear about it?"

"I may be from the slums a Glasgow, son, but I ken how tae read a newspaper."

"Sorry. I really didn't mean . . ."

"Ach, go on. I'm just takin' the piss oot ya, son." She laughed.

"It's sort of important that I speak with her."

Mrs Wallace poured us both a second cup of tea. "I dinnae ken who ya are, lad. Ya might be someone Kate wid like tae talk tae. But then ya might not be. I'm no glaiket tae what's been goin' on. Wee Kate's in some kind a bother an' I'm goin' off ma heid wi' worry." Mrs Wallace's voice began to splinter at the edges. She took a bite from a jam cake and stared down into her cup as if it might hold some answers.

"Maybe I can help her," I said.

She looked up. A sparkle returned to her eyes. "Aye. Maybe ya can."

"Will you tell me where I can find her, Mrs Wallace?"

"I could, but I dinnae think I better."

"What? I thought you just said . . ."

"I said I wasny a daft old cow, that's what I said."

"I never implied . . ."

"I ken that, son. Look, I'll tell ya what I can do."

"Yes."

"Muirhouse may no' be such a bonnie place tae stay, but it's near the Forth. Why dinnae ya take yoursel' for a wee walkaboot doon there. By the stone pier that goes oot tae Cramond Island. It used tae be one o' Kate's favourite places tae go. I used tae take the weans there mysel' when they were young. You go doon there an' wait. An' while you're waitin' I'll contact Kate an' tell her what ya told me. If she wants tae talk wi' ya, I'll tell her where tae find ya."

I smiled and nodded my head. Mrs Wallace had style. I liked that. I told her I would wait at the stone pier. I swallowed the last of my tea and rose to go to the door. Mrs Wallace told me a few more things about why Glasgow was a better place than Edinburgh as she was seeing me out.

"An they've no' got anything like the Barras in this town, either," she said. "Have ya no' been tae the Barras, son? Me an' the old yin used tae go every Sunday when the weans were small. You could get everything in the Barras. Just everything. Not like here."

It was still spitting down when I reached ground level and started walking toward the Forth. Tiny bubbles again. "We're merely the bubbles in the champagne of life," I muttered, almost audibly. The leaden grey, ponderously pensive sky made me say that. It's one of nature's imperatives.

I turned and looked back at Muirhouse before I left the estate. "Champagne of life?" I thought. I stepped off the kerb and started toward the beach. A new Citröen rolled slowly into the intersection and turned. Lost, I wondered, or just slumming?

CHAPTER TWENTY

It took me twenty minutes to reach the wide asphalt footpath that follows the shoreline of the Firth of Forth. I could see Cramond Island through the mist, but just barely. It seemed to be tentatively attached to the mainland by a series of unconnected cement pillars. A more solid pier joined the pillars just beyond a flagpole at the end of the path.

On the side of the path away from the Firth is a hilly meadow. It was wet and green and quiet. In the stroll between the car-park located behind me, on a raised terrace, and the flagpole in front of the pier, the only sound that disturbed the quiet was the squawk from an occasional gull. It was not a day for children to play in the little sandy strands along the shore. A few elderly folk taking their dogs for a stroll were the only signs of life. Them and a beach-tanned jogger wearing a tee-shirt that said "UCLA". I saw no one else.

I reached the stone pier and walked across its large, uneven paving stones to the sign warning Cramond Island was cut off during high tide. When the tide is out the pier and the stone pillars form a causeway to the island. Below the sign there was a tide-table that told when it was safe to walk out to the island.

I walked to the end of the pier and looked across the water, trying to see the coast of Fife. But I couldn't even see Inchcolm or Inchmickery, the two small islands just beyond Cramond. In fact, Cramond itself was growing dimmer in the grey granite mist.

I turned and began walking back in the direction I had come. I walked for fifteen minutes or so before turning around and retracing my steps towards the pier. Just killing time. I noticed a few more people along the path, including, again, the jogger from UCLA who was loping towards the car-park.

I stopped before I reached the stone pier and took out a smoke from my jacket. I popped a mint humbug into my mouth before lighting the tobacco. I threw the match away and watched a dog chase a stick his master had thrown into the water. People love to see dogs jumping into water making fools of themselves.

I felt something poke me gently in the back. I wheeled around and went into a crouch. I wasn't taking any chances. A young woman wearing a hooded anorak was standing in front of me.

"Hi," she said. "Are you the man my mother told me about?"

I relaxed and smiled. It was the way she said it. "Yes. Yes I am. My name is Rocco. I'm a friend of Morag Blair's."

She nodded. Her eyes darted from side-to-side like they were looking for something. Or someone. "What is it you want from me?" she said. There was fear in her voice as well as her eyes.

"I'd just like to talk to you about what's been happening." I pointed in the direction of the pier. "Can we walk?"

She stepped off without saying anything. I followed. She stepped down from the asphalt path to the coarse, sandy beach. Again I followed. We didn't say anything for a while. I just looked at the sand and the beach grass. I saw some tansy and sea rocket growing in the sand. And a mugwort. My kind of flower. I remember back in San Francisco I once took a nature hike with the Sierra Club along Baker Beach. The guide pointed out a mugwort and described it as "a common invader of wasteland". Sounded metaphorical to me then. The past couple of days made it sound more like biography.

"Why did you leave the show?" I asked after a few minutes.

"I had to," she replied. Her voice was steady and unemotional.

"Because of the heat put on you by the Home Office?"

"What?"

"The script. Because the Home Office wanted you to get a copy of the script for them."

"She stopped walking and turned so that she was facing me. "Who told you that?"

"Pete Swallow. That's why you had the row with Perez, wasn't it?" I broke off abruptly, realizing I had really put my foot in it. I mean it's one thing for a detective to question people. That's his job. But it's quite another to provide them with the answers. I was acting like a rank amateur. It wasn't the first time in my life.

"There were many reasons to row with Rodrigo," she said diplomatically.

"What were the others?"

Kate bent down and picked up a handful of small rocks and began tossing them into the Forth one at a time. "What do you want from me?" she said, with her back to me.

"Just some answers, that's all."

"Why? Why do you need answers? Why don't you just leave me alone? Why doesn't everybody just leave me alone?" She threw the rest of the stones in a single heave and began running toward the pier.

I called out after her, but she didn't stop. I started after her and caught her less than a hundred yards later. I put my hands on her shoulders. "Kate," I said, looking straight into her eyes. "You've got to start trusting somebody. Why not start with me? You can trust me. I might be able to help."

She looked down into the sand. "I just want to be left alone. I want to get this all behind me so I can get on with my life."

"A man has been murdered and a woman kidnapped. And if it means anything, I've had my life threatened twice. I want to get on with my life, too, Kate. I want to get to the bottom of this mess so we all can get on with our lives. I think you can help me do that. Will you help me do that, Kate?"

She looked up into my face. There were tears in her eyes. "I don't know what I can do. So many people have been hurt."

She started to walk again. I spun her round by the shoulders to stop her, then I put my arms around her to reassure her. I could feel her shoulders rise and fall as she continued sobbing quietly. I stood back to look at her. I wanted to suggest we go some place for a cup of tea.

She looked up at me. An expression of pain and puzzlement riveted her face. She started going limp in my grasp. Her lips began to form a word, but it never got out. She slumped in my arms. I could feel a sticky wetness on the back of her anorak. She fell to the sand. My hand was covered with blood.

I looked around. Two men with dogs no more than a hundred yards away were staring at me. Pointing at me. Further away, I saw the jogger with the UCLA tee-shirt. He was running up the path towards a man who was standing at the edge of the car park. The jogger was carrying something in his hand. Something in a case.

Kate was lying at my feet. Her eyes were locked open staring at nothing. The two men with the dogs were shouting. They started running toward me. I felt sick. The urge to lay down in the wet sand and wait for the tide to come and claim me was overwhelming. But I couldn't do it. I wiped my blood-soaked hand in a clump of grass and then started running. I had no idea where I was going.

CHAPTER TWENTY-ONE

I ran as hard as I could for as long as I could. "You can trust me! You can trust me! You can trust me!" I repeated it rhythmically. Spat it out like a terrible oath. It paced me and pushed me on.

"You can trust me!" It was an obscenity that grew more and more perverse each time I uttered it. "You can trust me!" I made myself a promise as I was running that if I got out of this jam alive, I would never say that again. To women in danger. To anyone!

I was somewhere in well-heeled Cramond when I stopped running. I bent over and gasped for breath. The pain in my chest was sharp and total. I felt like I had just been forced to smoke fifty cigarettes one after another while someone like Michelle rained short, hard jabs into my solar plexis.

I wheezed and snorted, sounding a lot like my old '61 Buick just before it threw a rod. After a few minutes of that my breathing began to return to normal and I could stand up straight. I walked until I came to a main road and caught the first bus back to the centre of town.

I got off on Lothian Road and went into Lanzio's for a cappuccino and a think. It was not yet lunchtime so the place was fairly empty. I took a table at the rear. I nodded and said "buongiorno" to the four Italian lads seated at the table opposite the big pizza oven. They were there whenever I went in. Or at least four young men smoking cigarettes and speaking Italian were. I often

111

wished that I knew what they were talking about. But not today. I had too many other things on my mind.

Like what do I know? No doubt, I would be wanted for murder very shortly. Those two men with the dogs and poor, dear Mrs Wallace could fit me up quite nicely. And who could blame them? Who would believe Kate was killed by a jogger wearing a UCLA tee-shirt?

Then there was Kate herself. Why would anyone want to kill her? She had had a row with Perez and left the company which sprung a very big leak in his production of *Ships in the Night*. His murder was the blast that sunk it.

Those were the thin facts of the case. Did the Home Office or MI6 snuff her for failing to obtain the script from Perez? On the surface, that didn't seem too likely since once they forced her to leave the show, they had accomplished a major part of their goal — shutting down the play. Was there a stand-in actress? Maybe Kate had changed her mind and was planning to return to the show? But what good would that do with Perez dead?

I could tell this was going to be a two cappuccino affair. I ordered a bowl of minestrone to go with them. Lanzio's serves a good bowl. Not a great bowl, but a good bowl. In the same league as Aunt Gina's, but rather further down in the tables.

The key to everything, as I saw it, was to try to suss out why Kate Wallace left the show and disappeared in the first place. She seemed quite surprised when I jumped the gun and regurgitated the story Pete Swallow told me.

Something she said stuck with me. "There were many reasons to row with Rodrigo." Those were her exact words. What were the other reasons? Were they important? Did they have anything to do with his murder and her disappearance, and ultimately, her own death?

So many questions. So few answers. I left the table to

make a phone call. I now had to speak to Swallow and Lily Montevideo more than ever. Michelle answered the phone and burned my ear for a few seconds before telling me that Pete didn't come back last night and Lily left early in the morning without saying a word.

"I don't know whether to shit or go blind," she said. "You know what I mean? Nobody around here tells me anything." She laughed.

"Well, I've got something else to tell you that isn't nearly so funny."

"Yeah?"

"Kate Wallace is dead."

"What?" Michelle shouted, nearly taking off my ear.

"She was killed. I was with her when it happened. Someone shot her."

A long silence followed on the other end of the line. If you didn't count the heavy breathing. Then she tried to speak, but only halting sounds came out. Sounds of hurt and anger.

"I'm sorry, Michelle," I said, after a while.

"Aw, hell. What do you know?"

"I know that Kate was frightened. And that she was your friend."

"Yeah. She was." Her voice trailed off.

"Where are they, Michelle?"

"Who?"

"Lily and Pete."

"I told you. I don't fucking know! I really don't."

"Maybe we should get together and talk. What do you say?"

"Talk? Talk about what?"

"Kate."

"I don't know what good it will do."

"Maybe none. But she was your friend."

"Aw, shit! Don't make it any worse. You don't know anything about it. Not a goddamn thing! I know what you're trying to do and I don't need your sympathy." She paused a moment and cleared her throat. "Hell, I don't know. I guess I wouldn't mind talking about it. Even with a putz like you. Get your ass over here before I go and change my mind."

"Fifteen minutes?"

"Yeah. Get goin'."

I hung up the phone and returned to my table. I took the last swallow of my lukewarm cappuccino and paid.

Out on Lothian Road I looked around for a cab. It's true what they say. There's never one when you want it. I had just made the decision to walk the half-mile to the hotel when I felt something at my elbow. I turned around to see a pale-looking man in a blue suit.

"Will you please come with me sir?" he said, politely. "There are some people who would like to talk with you."

"You from the *Patagonian Princess*?" I asked?

He ignored me and pointed to a dark-grey Citroën idling at the kerb. "This way, sir. It won't take long."

"What won't take long? You the guys with the cocaine?"

"Please, sir. All will be explained to you." He put his hand into the middle of my back the way only a professional knows how.

"Yeow!" I shouted. "Okay, okay. Why didn't you say so?" I walked to the kerb, opened the door and hopped in. So much for the rule about never accepting rides from strangers.

But then, not all of them were strangers. One of them was the short, dark man in the tropical shirt. Colonel Vega. The others I'd never seen before. But we didn't exactly have a chance to get acquainted. One of them took out a cloth soaked with something and put it under my nose. I went out like a small candle in a Florida hurricane.

114

When I came to I found myself in a wooden chair in the middle of any anonymous looking office. There were filing cabinets near a window that had its shade pulled. There was a large table near a wall. Around the table were several chairs, all of them occupied.

Before my eyes had returned completely to focus someone handed me a glass of water and said, "Drink this." I did.

Then a man from one of the chairs got to his feet and walked towards me. "Feeling better, are we, mate?" he said, in strongly accented tones. He sounded like he might have done some of the voices for "Minder."

He bent over and stuck his face into mine. "You're in a spot of bother, squire," he said. He was leering like he had just taken a tumble in the straw with the vicar's wife. And I was the vicar.

"You had to kidnap and drug me and bring me here to tell me that?" I said. "I could've saved you the time. By the way, where is 'here'?"

"Now, why'd you go and top that pretty young bird?" he said, ignoring my question.

"Who are you guys, anyway?" I said, looking around the room.

"We're the blokes what got you, sunshine," the man said, turning to his mates. Everyone but me chuckled.

"I know the Colonel over there," I said, pointing with my eyes. "Last time I saw him he put a shooter up my hooter."

"No time for jokes, sunshine. We've got you stitched up for the murder of the lassie. It'll go easier on you if you show us a little cooperation."

"You the cops?"

"Like I told you, we're the blokes what got you."

"Well, if that don't take the biscuit. Here, I thought you lot were the mafia."

"Shut your gob and answer the Major's questions,"

115

one of the men in the chairs said, threateningly. The Major turned and glared at him.

"Major?" I said. "And that yobbo over there is a colonel. In DINA, so they tell me. What are you? Special Branch?" The Major wasn't talking. "No, you're Smiley's people, aren't you? MI6. How's that for an educated guess, Major?"

"You are in no position to be guessing about anything, my son. Other than maybe how you're going to spend your declining years in the nick."

"I thought all you guys were from Cambridge or Oxford and sounded like Alec Guinness. What did you do? Work your way up through the ranks? Poor boy from Fulham makes good. Is that it?"

"Shut up, you cheeky bastard!"

I turned to the delegation sitting at the table. "Any of you geezers got a smoke on you?"

The Major's nostrils flared. He reared back and slapped my face with his open hand. My head started ringing like a burglar alarm in a high crime area.

"And there's more where that came from, sunshine," he said, regaining his cool. He stood up straight and started pacing back and forth in front of me like he was auditioning for a role in the sequel to one of those TV pageants about the British Raj. The only thing missing was the riding crop.

I was beginning to lose my patience. I mean drug skibos with guns pointed at me, a cock-eyed story about a kidnapping with the joke being on yours truly, Morag lying in the hospital with her head in a sling, a human bulldozer with a nasty mouth and bad temper, Kate Wallace lying dead in the sand and now these comedians. I didn't like it. Not one bit. I made a mental note to do something about it . Sometime. Sometime when I wasn't the prisoner of Chilean and British intelligence.

"Let us review your predicament," said the Major.

"Left-wing play is cancelled when one of the actresses comes to her senses and slopes off leaving her mates holding the bag. Seditious drama has to be postponed. Actress goes into hiding fearing bolshevik reprisal from the comrades. Then you decide to flush her out and bring her back into the fold to save what's left of the show. When she refuses, you top her. We've got you bang to rights, sunshine. You're all stitched up." The Major stepped back and smiled.

"You're still sore that Philby got away, aren't you? I can tell."

"Bloody Yank!" The Major turned momentarily to the others. "Was in America once, you know. Bloody awful place. Armed thugs and poofters bleedin' running wild in the streets."

"Oh yeah," I shot back in nationalistic pique. "Well, at least we don't torture the citizenry with our food. These things you call sausages. Worse than electric irons on your genitals."

"Leave it out. Look, sunshine, you're a liability to us. A pain in the ass, as you lot would say. If you were one of our own, we could just throw you in the nick or the closest body of water, whichever was the more convenient. But the fact that you are a foreign national, well, that complicates things a bit. Now, we can still put you in the nick, or that nearby body of water, but we'd rather not. Not at this time. Unless you decide to give us any more stick. Call it an act of international good will. You know, hands across the water and all that."

The Major reached inside his coat and pulled out an envelope. "This is a plane ticket to America," he said. "One-way." He handed me the envelope. "A couple of the lads here will accompany you to the airport just in case you have any thoughts about changing your mind."

"Am I supposed to say thank you, or something?"

"You're supposed to bugger off, that's all." The Major

117

walked to the opposite end of the room. "One last thing," he said. "Did, uh, Miss Wallace say anything to you about a missing script prior to her unfortunate demise?"

I smirked. "You English give me a laugh. 'Unfortunate demise'. It's like that scene from *The Third Man*. Remember?"

"Did she tell you where the script is?"

"You know when Wilfred Hyde-White asks Joseph Cotten where he's staying in Vienna and Cotten says he was going to stay with his pal Harry Lime, but that Lime got killed and Wilfred says, 'Goodness, that's awkward'. And then Cotten comes back 'Is that what you say when someone dies, "Goodness, that's awkward" '?"

"Did she say anything to you? Do you know where the bloody script is?" The major's neck was turning the colour of cheap red wine.

"Wouldn't you like to know?"

"Don't be difficult. It won't wash here."

"Get stuffed!"

"Still the cheeky bastard, are we? I wouldn't push my luck if I were you, old son. You're skating on very thin ice." The Major smiled cynically. "Good day." He turned and starting walking towards the door, stopping briefly to say something to one of the men at the table he called Payne.

"That's British justice for you!" I called out after him. "Deport a punter who hasn't done anything more than to be in the wrong place at the wrong time and who wants nothing more than a chance to see a couple of shows at the Fringe. But when it comes to one of the biggest drug traffickers on two continents, well, then, he's a colleague. A fellow officer. No wonder Philby went over the wall. You stink, Major. You're worse than the sausages!" I was shouting. The Major never looked back. He left the room.

I looked at Colonel Vega sitting at the table. "Perez

didn't know the half of it, did he, Major!" I yelled after him.

Vega got to his feet and walked over to me. "You should get down on your knees and thank the Major," he said, in a voice that bordered on a snarl. "In my country I would have had you shot and your body dumped in a remote field." He turned and left through the same door the Major had exited. The other men from around the table followed him. One of them looked familiar.

"How are things at UCLA?" I called out after him. He turned and looked at me. His face said nothing, but his eyes were smiling. Laughing. I felt sick. I wanted to toss my lizzards.

CHAPTER TWENTY-TWO

The one the Major had called Payne and another one waited until everyone left. Then Payne motioned to me. I got up and walked to the door. Payne's friend opened it and the two of them escorted me down a long, dark corridor to a service lift.

No one said anything as the lift hummed and clattered up to our floor. The silence continued after we stepped into it and began our descent. There was plenty I wanted to say to them. To the Major and Colonel Vega. Like whatever was in Perez's script about British-Chilean collaboration was spot on and they were living proof of it. And that I would do everything I could to find the script and see to it that it got the widest possible publicity. And that I would take great personal satisfaction in exposing them and every other rat-bag involved in this murderous alliance. That's what I wanted to tell them. I could've, too. But I didn't. I figured if I said more than "boo" to them I might have my ticket cancelled. Metaphorically as well as literally. Besides, they'd probably just laugh in my face. I wasn't exactly in the strongest possible position do back up my threats. The way it stood now, the worst thing that was going to happen to me was unofficial deportation. I didn't like it, but what could I do? California, here I come.

The lift came to a wheezing halt at a darkened floor. Payne slid back the metal accordion door-guard and stepped out. I followed with Payne's partner emerging behind me. We walked down the dark and damp corridor, up a few steps and through a thick metal door which led to the outside. I had no idea where I was.

I looked around, but nothing seemed familiar. There was something in the air though. Something besides murder. I could smell the rich, sweet aroma that is layed down over the city almost daily by the several breweries that are still operating. It smells sweet, like molasses, and savoury, like cooked vegetables, at the same time. When I first came to town and took my initial noseful, it reminded me of the fresh green beans my grandmother used to prepare. She'd add a bit of bacon to the pot to make them sweeter. For weeks I was convinced that some unscrupulous Scottish entrepreneur had stolen my grandmother's recipe and was mass producing green beans boiled in water with a bit of bacon.

It is a smell that sometimes blankets the city. You can't escape it. Like the smell from the former stockyards in Chicago or the paper mills around Portland. It roams around the city like an itinerant fog looking for noses to fill. A lot of people hate it, but with me, when it tweaks my olfactories I'm ten years old again and playing in my grandmother's backyard an hour before supper.

But I was much older than ten, my grandmother lives in a convalescent hospital and hasn't had a backyard for fifteen years. And I had no idea when my next supper would be. I was on my way to the airport. To America. To moral oblivion.

We began crossing a large, weedy car-park when I heard a familiar voice. "Hey, shithead! You stood me up!" I stopped and turned. It was Michelle. She was fifty yards away. She had a canvas rucksack strapped on her back. I was going to speak, but the sharp object that Payne poked into my side talked me out of it. He told me to keep walking. I did.

Michelle didn't like that one bit. "Hey! You! Greaseball! I'm talking to you!"

I turned my head but kept walking. Michelle dropped her pack and was running towards us. Payne told me to tell her to go away. Sure. Might as well tell Neil Kinnock to compère a testimonial dinner for Arthur Scargill.

Michelle ran up and stood in front of the three of us. "What's the matter with you, shit-for-brains? Why'd you go and stand me up? You said you'd be over in fifteen minutes. I waited a goddamn hour for your mangey ass."

"Sorry," I said. "Something came up." I motioned with my eyes to the two book-ends.

"Fuck that, Jack!" Michelle was unsympathetic. "And who are these bozos? They look like pigs."

Payne was losing his patience. He turned to me. "Tell your girlfriend here you're in a hurry."

"Girlfriend!" Michelle shouted, loud enough to split wood. "You goddamn sexist moron! What the hell do you know about anything?"

Payne unbuttoned his jacket. I just knew he had a gun in there somewhere.

"They've got guns!" I yelled as I jumped on Payne's instep as hard as I could. He doubled over and began howling like a vampire with a toothache. But he still had the presence of mind to go for his gun.

I jumped away from the two men and looked at

Michelle. She stood there puzzled by it all. "They killed Kate!" I said.

Before the words were cool on my lips, Michelle spun around and delivered a karate kick to Payne's chest. His gun went flying and so did he. The other one caught it below the chin. He folded like a revival tent in a town full of atheists. She hit him again as he went down.

Payne had swiftly recovered and was coming at her. He smashed the side of her face with a large and angry fist. Michelle fell to the ground and hit her head. I countered with a kick that caught Payne in the groin. This just wasn't his day. He bent over holding his privates. He tried to scream but nothing came out. I drop-kicked him in the head sending him on a one-way trip to visit the sandman.

Michelle was back on her feet shaking her head like she was trying to jump-start it. It seemed to work. She looked around surveying the damage. "Not bad for a wimp," she said. Then she smiled and held out her hand for me to shake. "Who the hell are these creeps, anyway?"

"Later," I said. "Let's get out of here first." Michelle went and got her rucksack and then we ran until Payne and his pal were just a lousy memory.

We ducked into a cafe somewhere in the West End. I forget the name. Over a couple of steamy white coffees I told her about my interview with Smiley's people and convinced her that one of them had killed Kate Wallace.

"Poor Kate," she said. "She was just an innocent bystander."

"Yeah. So am I."

"Just another of Rodrigo's 'protégés'. Most don't end up dead, though. Just fucked up."

"What are you talking about?"

"Nothing, man."

"Michelle. What the hell's going on?"

She looked away. Her eyes wandered until they found a spot on the wall where they came to rest.

"Look," I said. "Is it so hard to level with me? Who knows who's going to be next on their list? After me, that is."

"Pete wants to talk to you," she said. "Tonight. He'll explain it all to you. Honest."

"What about Lily?"

"Pete will tell you everything. He said to meet him in the cafe at the Traverse. At 10.30."

"Will Lily be with him? I've got some questions I'd like to ask her."

Michelle rose from her seat. "Ten thirty. Be there." She turned and started to walk away.

"Michelle!" I called out.

She turned back to me. "What now?" She had a pained expression on her face.

"I'm really sorry about Kate."

Her eyes dropped to the floor. "Yeah. I know. Thanks, man." She wheeled around and walked out the door.

CHAPTER TWENTY-THREE

I spent the rest of the afternoon in a boozer on Broughton Street. The one Rudy likes to call 'The Shit and Shovel'. I nursed a couple pints and a few bags of crisps and tried to put it all together. It didn't fit. But I already knew that. Nothing fit. Nothing ever fit. And nothing ever seems like it really is. Those were the only things I knew for sure.

Rodrigo Perez murdered. Kate Wallace likewise. Lily Montevideo was maybe kidnapped by DINA or the

KGB. Or both for all I knew. There was a script. A hot number packed with political armalite. But nobody knew where to find it. And a lot of people seemed to want it. Bad.

Those were the facts. The other stuff was as grey as the stone they used to build the New Town. But Pete Swallow would sort it all out and set me straight, right? Fat chance!

My eyes wandered to the television screen above the bar. The Test Match was on. It was the third or fourth of the endless summer series.

Ian Botham was bowling. Ian Botham was always bowling. He'd taken a couple of wickets, but the other guys had rolled up 336 for six.

Cricket! What a game. A number of American writers and other people in the know have said that baseball, in particular, even sports in general, are a metaphor for American life. I'm not sure just what that means, but it seems to make some kind of subliminal, if not actual, sense.

Since I've been living in Britain I've tried to figure if cricket is a metaphor for British, or at least English, life. As a rank outsider, I could be cruel and say if it is a metaphor, life in "Old Blighty" must be slow, white and dull. But that's not fair. Cricket isn't a game, it's a process. A process where the defence puts up its best bowlers — it's off-spinners, leg spinners, fast bowlers, those that bowl googlies and those that don't. And the bowler, running, gliding, delivering the goods, doesn't so much try to get the batsman out, like the pitcher does in baseball, but rather wears him down with his relentless persistence. I mean, if you give up 336 runs, you can't be going for the quick kill. Americans go for the throat. The English try to finesse you and impress you with their tenacity. They take the long view. The historical view. It will all come to pass and good will out. Americans go for the double play and the strikeout. If they don't get it they lose interest.

Botham bowled out the seventh batsman. Leg-before-wicket. The bar patrons cheered and slapped each other on the back. The English side whooped it up, too, and crowded around Botham slapping him on the back. It had been some time since the last wicket fell. Like a week ago Monday or something.

But there is something fascinating about the game. You can leave a match, turn off the telly or radio and come back to it hours or days later and pick it up again like nothing happened. It remains. Sort of like the class struggle. There are dead times, uninteresting times when nothing much seems to be happening. But then a wicket is taken or somebody like Viv Richards or Gordon Greenidge reaches a double century and everything comes alive. The game, life, the universe itself is revealed. It all does have meaning. The Perez case needed a wicket, badly.

The crisps and beer were starting to bloat inside me. Someone other than Botham took another wicket. It looked like England would get to start their innings before long. I was becoming absorbed in the mopping-up operation taking place on the screen when a figure of a man came between me and the telly. It was Jocky.

"You're no' a cricket man," he said, jesting.

"A bit."

"Bloody English toffs runnin' around in more expensive breeks an' jumpers than the working class can afford ta wear ta kirk on Sunday."

"No argument there."

"So, what'll ya be drinkin', then, eh?"

"I'm still working on the last of this one, Jocky."

His face turned the colour of a cricket ball. "Whin a man offers ta buy ya a pint, yid be bloody well advised ta take it."

"Heavy."

"Aye. I thought so." Jocky padded off to the bar and returned with two pints. He sat down across from me and took a generous gulp of his lager. He sat his glass down on the table and leaned forward. "You're no' still sore at me fer the row we had t'other day, are ya, son?"

"It's ancient history."

"Aye. I widny like ta fall out wi' ya."

"Likewise."

"Even if ya are a daft bugger when it comes ta politics."

"Uh, oh. Are we going to start up again?"

"Ach, no. I'm just rabbitin' on. Have ya seen Rudy aboot?"

"Not since the last time I saw you."

"A braw lad, that yin."

"That's a fact."

"An' how yer makin' oot wi' that case ya was talkin' aboot?"

"The Perez thing?"

"Aye."

"I feel like I'm in a trench in no-man's land. All sides are tossing grenades in at me and they're going off in my lap."

"Then I guess ya heard what that actor lady said. The one whose husband was kilt. She's been spreadin' anti-Soviet lies in the newspaper."

"For once I'm inclined to agree with you, but I can't figure out why she's doing it."

"I'll tell ya why. Because the whole lot of 'em are nothin' but a load a middle class trendies an' feminists that hate the workin' class."

I smiled. "Simple as that, eh?"

"Aye. An' you should no' be makin' jokes aboot it, son. It's serious business, that."

"Too serious, I'm afraid, to be left to clichés, Jocky."

126

"You might as well be in cahoots wi' 'em yoursel'. You an' your bloody Trotskyite pals. Enemies of true socialism, the lot of yous."

"Jocky, please. I'm tired. Let's watch the Test match. Look. Botham's going for his fifth wicket."

"Sod yer fifth wicket! We're talkin' aboot a cowardly attack on the Soviet Union. Why do ya no' want ta talk about that, eh?"

"Well, why do you think she did it, then? Accuse the KGB. Did you know that Perez was attacked and beaten up by Stalinist goons in France two years ago?"

Jocky's eyes doubled their size. "Yer bloody hopeless, son," he said, rising from his chair. "I dinnae ken why I waste my time on ya."

"I do so appreciate being harangued by you. It's a dying art."

Jocky pointed a trembling finger at me. "I'll no' be stayin' at the same table wi' the anti-communist petit bourgeois. Ya git right up ma nose." He picked up his glass. "If ya want ta ken the truth, which I doubt very much, ya should be at Powderhall tonight."

"I'm going to learn the truth from a bunch of greyhounds?"

"Nae, ya dumplin'! I'll be there wi' one a ma comrades from the Soviet Union. I was in Spain wi' his feyther. He'll sort ya oot a'right. You'll no' be hearin' a pack a slanderous lies from him."

"I think I'd rather take my chances with the dogs."

"Ya just be there, eh?"

"Why not? Couldn't be any worse than what faces me at the Traverse. First race still go off at half-seven?"

"Aye. Ya ken Powderhall, then?"

"Yeah, I ken."

Jocky turned and walked to the bar. I could hear him starting up on England and the upper class nature of cricket. Then he bought all his pals a drink.

127

CHAPTER TWENTY-FOUR

It was 4 pm. The grey skies opened up a little and dumped some rain on the streets. Except for my slippery shoes, I didn't much care. I walked from the boozer to the Fringe Office to pick up another guide. I thought maybe there was something playing that could take my mind off things for a couple of hours.

Despite the drizzle, the area in front of the Fringe Office was crowded with people handing out soggy leaflets and people coming to and going from the ticket office. A thin man with dark, bushy hair and a beard passed me his leaflet. I read it. It announced that Ian Saville, "socialist conjurer", would be performing his new show *Brecht on Magic* as an added feature to the political cabaret. First, it was Mark Miwurdz and a few others. Then Roland and Claire Muldoon and The Left Wing Teds. Now, Ian Saville, a socialist magician! This was getting serious.

"A cross between Tommy Cooper and Leon Trotsky", the leaflet said. "See the labour theory of value explained by a rope trick." I fought the urge to join the queue and book my ticket right then and there. Sod all this other stuff. Powderhall, the KGB and Pete Swallow. They were ruining my Festival.

I looked at the queue for a long moment trying to decide if I were a man of conviction or not. But before I had a chance to find out I heard someone call out, "Hello! San Francisco." I turned my head. It was Waxlow of the *Mail*.

"Seen anything interesting?" he said, getting right to the point.

"Plenty," I replied. "But not at the Festival."

"My God, there is a lot of rubbish out there. If you're thinking of seeing Les Deux Kangareaux Flambeau, forget it."

128

"The what?"

"Some sappy comedians from Australia. They won a Perrier Award two years ago. Don't ask me how. No taste, no class, and above all, no talent."

"Sounds like my life the last couple of days."

"What's that?"

"Nothing. So, what do you recommend?"

"Couple of good items at Theatre Workshop. Theatre of the Eighth Day at Richard Demarco's venue. They're from Poland. And there's a bloke at the Netherbow doing *Confederacy of Dunces*. A one-man show with eighteen bloody parts! It's a *tour de force*. I wouldn't miss it."

"Right."

"How about you? What have you seen?"

"Oh, not much, really. Been spending most of my time following up on the Perez murder."

"Oh. Then you must be on your way to the press conference." My face must have been twisted into the question mark it felt like, for Waxlow looked at me like I had the intelligence of a plate of home-made stovies.

"You did hear about it, didn't you?"

"Well, I've been pretty busy these last few days."

"Then you didn't hear about the defection this morning?"

"Defection?"

"Yes. One of the actors from that Russian theatre company has sought protection from the British government."

"Protection? From the British government? He must be joking."

Waxlow frowned. "This is big news, old man. Even for California, I should think."

"And there's a press conference?"

Waxlow looked at his watch. "Yes. At the George Hotel in twenty minutes. I have a car if you want a lift."

I nodded. We hiked down the Royal Mile to Cockburn Street, where Waxlow had parked his car. On the way he told me the details, as he knew them, of the defection. Seems a young actor from the Meyerhold Theatre Company disappeared a few days ago. About the same time Perez was murdered. He surfaced this morning in the protective custody of the Edinburgh District Council. Why the Council and not some central government authority seemed strange to me. Waxlow didn't know why, either.

The lobby of the George was crawling with guys in dark suits with walkie-talkies pressed up against the sides of their heads. The the air was filled with tension. You could almost taste it. The room where the press conference was to take place had a security set-up that fell somewhere between an airport check-in and a strip search at San Quentin. Plus, you had to produce a press card. I had one that I made myself a long time ago. I never went anywhere without it. It got me into more places than a Tory in a dark-blue suit.

Waxlow and I took seats about half-way back among the dozen or so rows of soft, plush chairs.

I never saw so many bright lights, cameras and wires. It looked like the set of a Steven Spielberg extravaganza. I half-expected E.T. to come waddling in from the wings and take a seat at the long table in the front which had microphones arranged on it like a large bouquet of stainless steel flowers with electrical cord stems.

After a few minutes some men came out. They looked a lot like the kind that worked for the Major and Colonel Vega. Then three more men emerged and took seats at the table. Flashbulbs went off, video lights went up and I nearly went blind.

I recognized one of the men at the table. He was a leader of the Labour-dominated District Council. I heard him speak several times at rallies during the miners' strike. He opened with a few words about who was seated at the table with him and then turned the proceedings over to them.

One of them introduced the other man as Alexi Tarkov, the defecting Russian. He said that although Tarkov spoke English rather well, he would be reading from a prepared text in his native Russian. He himself was there to translate Tarkov's words into English.

Then Tarkov began reading from his text. He looked and sounded terrified. The papers in his hands shook violently, distracting everybody including himself. He laid them on the table and leaned forward. After he read a paragraph or so, the man next to him would translate the words into English. This format continued until the young Russian had completed his statement.

"My name is Alexi Tarkov," he began. "I am an actor. I have been performing with the Meyerhold Theatre for more than six years. After a long and painful searching of my soul, I have decided to seek the protection of the progressive-minded government of the city of Edinburgh, Scotland.

"I have made the decision to leave my beloved country and my friends and colleagues because I can no longer continue to live an artistic and political lie in the Soviet Union. I am an actor and a communist, but I have found it impossible to live honestly as either in my homeland. I am a political artist. I cannot live in a place where both art and politics are held in bondage.

"I shall seek to pursue my career and my beliefs outside the Soviet Union, knowing full well the risks and difficulties I will encounter. I hope to work and live the kind of life exemplified by the late and great Rodrigo Perez, whose tragic death here in Edinburgh hastened my decision."

When Tarkov finished his statement, he looked at his translator and then rose from his chair and left the table.

131

Howls in the form of questions nipped at his heels as he disappeared through a side door. The translator said there would be "no questions at this time", something which was obvious even to me. A collective sigh went up from the gallery. Those who didn't sigh continued to ask their questions. Shout their questions. It was like the floor of the Stock Exchange fifteen minutes from the closing bell. Only when the translator and the councillor left the table did the show end and the noise abate.

"Well, what do you make of that?" said Waxlow. He sounded puzzled.

"I think the tabloids have been thrown a curve."

"A what?"

"It's a baseball term."

"Oh, of course. What does it mean in English?"

"It means that Fleet Street is going to have a very hard time taking this one to the bank. No anti-Soviet gold to mine here."

"That seems fairly obvious."

"I doubt it will even make the front pages. Check it out. A Russian who is a socialist defecting from the Soviet Union because he can't practice his beliefs is something the tabloids won't understand."

"Do you think the whole thing might be a hoax?"

"See what I mean?"

"Actually, no. What was that chap really on about, anyway?"

"It's too complicated even for much of the left to understand. I can't begin to explain it to the *Mail*."

"Well, no matter. I better file my story. Maybe I can spice it up a bit, but you're right about it being confusing. Probably rates a box on page three. Little more."

"Next to the nude?"

"Maybe above. Depends on how it's rewritten in London."

"Does it ever get to you, Waxlow?"

"What?"

"The *Mail*. The *Sun*. The *Mirror*."

"You can't think about that. It's a job. A good job and that's all I think about."

"Yeah."

"Bit interesting, that chap mentioning Perez, don't you think?"

"Yeah. Very."

Waxlow looked at his watch. "Well, I'm off. A new Wexler piece is being performed at, where is it?" He flipped some pages in his notebook. "Ah, yes. The Cornerstone. Jeannie Fisher. It's a one-woman play. I always find Wexler interesting even if I don't agree with him much of the time." Waxlow rose from his chair. I walked out with him. "We must get together for drinks before it's all over," he said. "I'd really like to hear about California."

"Sure," I said. I watched him walk through the lobby and out the entrance to the hotel. I just hung around for a while looking at people.

About ten minutes later the district councillor who had been at the press conference whisked right past me on his way to the street. I called out his name.

He stopped and turned. "No questions," he said. "Please."

"I'm not a reporter."

"Oh. Then who are you? What do you want? I'm in a terrible hurry."

"I'm associated with Teatro Jara. I'm working for Pete Swallow."

"What kind of work is that?"

"I'm a private investigator from California."

His face relaxed and he smiled. "I thought you were an American. I have a cousin who stays in Seattle. Is that near where you stay?"

133

"About a thousand miles."

"Oh. I really am in a hurry. I've got a Housing Committee meeting at six."

"I have a couple of questions about the defector. They'll only take a minute."

The councillor looked at his watch. "I really must be going. If you want to ride up to the chambers with me, we can talk on the way."

"It's a deal."

We walked out of the hotel. The councillor hailed a cab. The ride was only five minutes, but I learned a lot. He told me that Tarkov showed up at Labour Party headquarters, seeking asylum, the morning following the Perez murder. The councillor said he received a call from party headquarters and rushed down to talk to him.

The young Russian had told him that he had been trying to make contact with Perez since the day he arrived in Edinburgh, but was unable to get away from the watchful eyes of the KGB. He told the councillor he simply wanted to talk with Perez. About politics, the theatre, things like that. On the night of the murder, Tarkov had finally slipped out of his hotel without the KGB on his tail. Or, so he thought. He went over to the George Hotel to see Perez. When he got there he saw him leaving with a woman.

Tarkov then followed the couple, trying to get up the courage to speak to Perez. He followed them all the way up to Calton Hill where he encountered three dudes from the KGB. They had words and a scuffle broke out. The KGB men tried to subdue him and take him back to the hotel, but Tarkov managed to escape them. He spent the night at the Youth Hostel near the Netherbow. In the morning he saw the headlines in the newspaper. That's when he decided to jump and went to the Labour Party headquarters.

I asked the councillor if I could talk to Tarkov. He

said that would be impossible. I pleaded. He said it was still impossible. He told me that following the press conference he had been taken into protective custody by "representatives of the Home Office". The Major, no doubt. Or some of his colleagues.

The councillor shook my hand and told me to look up his cousin in Seattle when I returned home to California and then left for his Housing Committee meeting. Me, I had to go to the dog track and meet some Russian who would "sort me out" about the Perez murder. It was my luck that it was the wrong Russian.

CHAPTER TWENTY-FIVE

Powderhall is between Broughton Road and the Water of Leith, right in the middle of a small industrial area and hard by a DIY store and the regional rubbish-treatment plant. It's a place punters can spend an evening without emptying their wallets. I mean the most popular betting window takes 10p wagers.

I'd gone there regularly for a short time last year. Hung out with the high rollers at the 50p window. I had to quit, though. I was beginning to lose too much money. Besides, Annie told me I was starting to talk out of the side of my mouth.

And here I thought I had it all figured out. A friend of mine from Frisco we call Barry Bay-Meadows blew into town one Saturday on the winnings he made off the nags. Parlayed a couple forecasts into four figures. He gave me a few tips and ruffled some large denomination notes under my nose. That's the way you get bit. I would've quit after the first couple of times, but I noticed that the first and second place finishers were coming out of trap number six with alarming frequency. So, I thought there was a system to be devised. I went to the *Evening News-Scotsman* building and looked up the results for the past month and, sure enough, the dog coming out of the number six trap won or placed a little over fifty per cent of the time. The next best finisher was the dog in the number four trap.

Simple, right? I figured I had cracked the betting nut mathematically. Bet six to win and place and a six-four forecast reversed in nearly every race. Lost nearly every race, too. Got to the point when I went to the 50p window, the clerk would roll her eyes and punch in the numbers without even asking. But, like I said, I had the will power to quit. Annie helped. She'd take me for long drives in the country on race nights. That was months ago. I'm completely cured now. However, I must admit that Tuesdays, Thursdays and Saturdays are not quite the same.

I paid my £1.20p and passed through the ancient turnstile into the grandstand. I took the racing programme as a matter of habit and, for the same reason, stopped by the scratches board. It was 7.15 and the grandstand was only thinly populated, regulars poring over their programmes trying to suss out the winning combinations that would at least pay for a round of drinks.

I walked by the betting windows without turning my head and on to the Silver Hound Bar. There I saw Jocky standing at one of the rails that looks out over the track. He had two or three pals of his own age with him. There was a younger man, too. He was wearing a suit and stood rather stiffly near Jocky's elbow. I walked over.

"Who do you like in the first race?" I said to his back.

He turned around. "What?" He broke into a smile. "Oh, it's you, is it? Found yer bottle and decided to come, did ya? Good lad. There still may be a wee bit a hope fer ya."

"This the bloke ya was tellin' us aboot, Jocky?" said one of Jocky's mates.

"Aye. Calls himself Rocco." He made a sweeping gesture with his arm. "This lot here is Jimmy, Angus an' Dave. And this one is Yuri Maximov from the Soviet Union." He put his hand on Maximov's shoulder. "I've known this yin since he was a wee lad. Known his father forever. We bashed the neeps for the Last Supper."

I shook hands with all of them and exchanged brief greetings. An awkward moment of silence followed, which was broken by the man introduced as Dave.

"Here come the hounds," he said. All eyes were relieved to regroup on the track, and the six dogs and their handlers who were leading them around the track. It meant the first race was less than five minutes away.

"I fancy number five," said Dave. "Look at those times. 28.97, 28.95, 28.90," he said, reading from the dog's previous race record from the programme.

"Trouble is finding the right combination," said Jocky. "Bettin' on five will pay bugger all. He's the favourite. Yi've got ta git the winnin' forecast. I'm goin' wi' number two. I've been followin' him for two weeks. I think he's goin' ta come in tonight."

"Two?" said Jimmy. "Ya must be daft. He hasny come in better than fourth in his bloody life."

"I got ma mind made up," said Jocky defensively.

"What dee ya say, young yin?" Jimmy said to me. "Dee ya ken the dogs?"

"I'd put 50p on number six," I said, with the arrogance of a person who knew what he was talking about.

"Six?" said Dave, looking at his programme. "That poor bastard disny have a time under 29.15. He'll be lucky if he comes in before they start the second race." Everybody laughed except Yuri Maximov who was looking through a pair of binoculars in the direction of the track.

"You serious about number six, laddie? asked Jimmy. "Or are ya jist havin' us on?"

"If you look at the statistics . . ." I started to say.

"Statistics!" Jimmy repeated. He turned to his pals and laughed. "You know Molly?" he asked rhetorically.

"Aye," said Dave.

"The girl who works the 50p window?" asked Angus.

"Aye," nodded Jimmy, giggling. "She's married ta ma cousin. You know, Rab. He sometimes drinks at the pub." The other men nodded their heads.

"Rab Forsyth," said Jocky. "He used ta be a party man back in the fifties.

"Aye. That's the one," said Jimmy. "Well, Molly told me once about this daft bloke who used ta come up ta her window an' bet on the number six dog every bloody race. Didny matter if the poor bugger had four legs or three he'd bet jist the same. Told her he had worked it out statistically." Jimmy roared with laughter. The others joined in. Even Yuri Maximov giggled. I tried to crawl under a pint glass.

"Aye," Jimmy continued. "A real nutter, that yin. I think Molly said he was a Yank. Ya widny ken who it was, wid ya, son?"

"No. I widny ken," I said trying to sound as non-American as I could.

"We better place our bets, lads," said Dave. "The dogs are linin' up." All except Jocky and Maximov rose and headed for the 10p window.

"I'll put 10p on number six fer ya, son," said Jimmy, laughing out loud. I smiled. Jocky gave Dave 40p to reverse a 20p forecast for him.

When the three men left for the betting window, Jocky turned to me. "I was wi' Yuri's feyther in Spain," he said, slapping Maximov on the back. I felt the urge to ask him if they fought the fascists or the anarchists, but it passed.

"Yuri is with the Soviet theatre company that's performin' at the Festival," he continued.

"An actor?" I said, looking at Maximov.

"Nae. He isny an actor. He's a member of the party. Political adviser for cultural affairs. He protects the artists from political and physical attacks by the class enemy."

"Oh. KGB. Why didn't you say so?"

"You say that with obvious distaste," said Maximov coolly.

"Not at all. It's just that political police tend to rub me the wrong way, that's all. Sorry if I offended. You see. I've had some rather nasty run-ins with them recently."

"Ach, ya never," said Jocky. "See, Yuri, I told ya he was a bloody Trotskyite. Or anarchist. I never could figure oot just which."

"Jocky! You promised you wouldn't tell." I smiled at him. I admit it was a sarcastic smile.

"Ach! Yer bloody hopeless. Tell him, Yuri. Ta set the bloody record straight. Rocco here is workin' on the murder of that Perez bloke. Tell him the Soviet Union hadny a thing ta do wi'it."

Maximov cleared his throat. "You must be referring to that unfortunate statement in the press made by the Montevideo woman. As a representative of the Soviet government, I categorically deny the false allegations made by her. They are wildly irresponsible and only serve to fuel the anti-Soviet hysteria whipped up by the West."

"There," said Jocky. "if that disny satisfy ya, then bugger all will."

"Look. If I want an official statement, I'll read it in the papers. What I want to know is why Lily Montevideo made those charges if they weren't true."

Maximov shrugged his shoulders. "I do not know. I

am not a psychiatrist. Perhaps she is allied with Western intelligence."

"I think we can put that one in trap number six with the three-legged dogs. Do you know who Perez and Montevideo are?"

"Yes, I do."

"Petit bourgeois dilettantes," chimed Jocky, draining the last from his pint glass. "Anti-Soviet smart arses. They were no' a friend of the workin' man."

I turned to Maximov. "Do you agree with Mr Stalin here?"

Maximov smirked. "I would perhaps choose different words, but my friend is essentially correct. Mr Perez and Miss Montevideo seemed to have carved out quite a career in the West with their anti-socialist theatre."

"Aye!" added Jocky, "that's the bloody truth, that is."

"Maybe anti-Soviet," I said,"but not anti-socialist. There is a great distinction."

"I think not," said Maximov. His tone was as cold as a greyhound's nose.

"Well," I said,.. "I don't want to stand here and argue with the KGB. I may make lousy bets on the dogs, but I'm not a cluck." Maximov smiled. "But purely for the sake of discussion and nothing else, let's look at a scenario. I'm not saying I believe it, mind you, but it does make a certain amount of sense."

"Ach! You an' yer bloody scenarios," said Jocky with disgust.

I looked at Maximov. "May I?"

"If you wish," he replied dispassionately.

"Okay. Perez is an anti-communist, anti-Soviet nogoodnik. Slanderer of bolshevism, Stalinism, Brezhnevism, rheumatism. You name it. Stepped on a lot of red shoes in his day. Maybe stepped too hard. The word goes out from the politburo or Moscow Centre, 'Let's chill this bastard'. Strike a blow for international proletarian unity. Stuff like that. Perfect set-up is the Edinburgh Festival. He'll be there. You'll be there. In fact, everybody will be there. The place is sure to be lousy with folk who'd like to see him take a long walk on a short pier with an iron haggis tied around his neck. Especially with all that noise from the Home Office right up his nose. Perfect set up to settle some old political scores. Hell, man, I saw *The Fairly Red Flag*. He gave you lot a bloody good hiding. I could see you sending a couple comrade-blasters up to Calton Hill to send him on a one-way trip to that gulag in the sky. What do you think?"

Maximov took out a cigarette from a pack he had in his suit jacket. A Marlboro. He tapped it on the crystal of his watch and put it into his mouth and lit it with an expensive looking lighter. "Perhaps it makes sense to you," he said, "but it bears no resemblance to the truth."

"Well, then, hip me to it, man. The simple truth is all I'm looking for."

"Your scenario is crude. Something one might find in one of the British tabloids. Or an American movie."

"No one is perfect."

"Hold yer wheesht!" demanded Jocky.

"I will admit that there is very little sorrow on my part that Mr Perez has passed from the scene of contemporary theatre. I personally found the great majority of his work offensive to me as a socialist." I wanted to laugh in his face, but I held my wheesht.

"But," he continued, "I would have preferred to have him exposed and rejected by the working class, not brutally murdered. That is not a political solution. Not a Soviet solution to deal with someone like Mr Perez. Besides, he was but a minor irritant. A very minor irritant, indeed. We have your Mr Reagan and his Star Wars weapons system to contend with. It is a somewhat slightly larger problem. No, my friend, no one in the

141

Soviet Union had the slightest interest in harming your Mr Perez, much less killing him."

"Well, it's your word against Lily Montevideo's. And I know her political credentials. She is a revolutionary artist. You. You're just a guy in an expensive suit I met at the dog track."

"That is your opinion," said Maximov. "I am not responsible for that." He turned up the corners of his mouth to form a condescending smile. I didn't much care for it.

"The name Alexi Tarkov ring a bell?" I asked.

The muscles in Maximov's neck turned to steel wire and the colour drained from his face. "Why do you mention that name?" he said finally.

"I just came from his press conference. He was up on Calton Hill the night Perez got bumped off. At the very same time and the very same place. A couple of your lads were there, too. They tried to shanghai Tarkov. They might have done a lot more."

"Who's this bloody Tarkov, then?" Jocky asked.

Maximov turned to him. "He is a member of the Meyerhold Theatre. He was kidnapped three days ago by British and Chilean intelligence. I have no doubt he was tortured and drugged. What your friend here witnessed was the product of that torure and drugging."

"The bloody bastards!" Jocky spit.

"He sounded perfectly normal to me," I said. "Scared, but normal."

"Imperialist lies! The West is absolutely hysterical when it comes to these cases of so-called defection. The imperialists are so totally bankrupt that they must stage-manage these elaborate charades in order to discredit the Soviet Union. It is cynical and hypocritical, not to mention criminal. I believe kidnapping is still a punishable crime in the west."

"What you say is absolutely correct. Most of the time.

But it is not a catechism to be recited. It doesn't apply to this case, I'm afraid."

"Oh."

"No. Tarkov said he was a practising communist and that one of the reasons he was leaving the mother country was for its betrayal of socialism."

"Bloody Trotskyite!" shouted Jocky. "They're everywhere. He should be shot!" His face was the colour of a cricket ball again.

"Another reason for leaving, eh?"

"Ya daft bugger. Yer talkin' a load a shite!"

Maximov stood by, cool as a winter day in Murmansk. "I do not choose to argue with you, my friend. The Soviet Union had nothing to do with the murder of Rodrigo Perez."

"Back to official denials, eh? It doesn't wash, Maximov. You'll have to do better than that."

"Answer me this, my smart friend. If we killed Perez, why would we not have also killed Miss Montevideo? Whatever you may think of the KGB, you must surely give us more credit than to kill Perez and then kidnap his wife only to allow her to escape so she could publicly accuse us of these highly charged crimes. Not even your CIA is that stupid."

It was my turn to pause and light up a cigarette. The smoke that escaped through my nostrils following the first puff carried with it a lot more than simply carcinogenic fumes. I could see it trying to dissipate into the atmosphere, searching for a place to hide. Disappear. Forget. First time in my life I ever identified with cigarette smoke.

Yeah, the Russian was right. I guess I knew all along that the KGB was being framed for Perez's murder. Not that they weren't capable of it, but it just wasn't their style. Not for someone like Perez. A diplomat, a defector, a CIA agent, a Lech Walesa. Maybe. But not a playwright. Maximov was right. Perez was only a minor irritant to the Soviets. But that's not what really put the poison pellet into the leg of my scenario. It was what he said about Lily Montevideo. It would indeed take a real chowderhead to think that the KGB would kill Perez and let Montevideo live to tell the press about it. What was really depressing was the obvious fact that no one would. KGB, DINA, CIA, MI6. Unless, of course, you were simple-minded enough to believe Swallow's story that she escaped her captors. Eyewash. That's what that was.

I guess more than anything. I was trying to give Lily Montevideo the benefit of my own doubts. I wanted to believe the KGB kidnapped her and killed Perez, not because of any self-motivated hatred of Stalinism and its political bully boys, although there's enough of that around to stretch from Barcelona to Gdansk and back again, but because I wanted to believe she was telling the truth. That she was sticking to her principles of telling it like it was and letting the chips fall where they may, no matter whose floor they fell on. That was what had characterized the work of Perez and Montevideo for nearly two decades. Gave it integrity.

But Maximov put the blast on that. An officious, insinuating piece of work who had about as much in common with socialism as comrade General Jaruzelski, he had nevertheless cleared up some things for me. Narrowed the possibilities. For that I owed him my thanks. But I offered him only a smoke instead. He looked right through me and took out his pack of Marlboros. I didn't mind. I wasn't battling the personification of "Darkness at Noon", just a functionary of the state in a Bond Street suit. Winning or losing this face-off really didn't matter to me. We just stood there quietly loathing each other.

Jocky broke in. "There!" he said. "I hope that'll knock some sense inta that heid a yers. I told ya Yuri wid sort ya oot."

Before I could think of something sarcastic to say, Jocky's pals returned carrying drinks and pound notes.

"Here ya go, ya lucky bastard," said Dave, handing over two one pound notes and some change to Jocky. "Ya won the forecast."

"How did number six do?" I asked.

Jimmy laughed." I owe ya an apology, son," he said. "Yer dog came in fifth." Everybody laughed, including me.

I stayed around for the next race talking with Jocky and his pals about dogs. Dave told stories about the early days of flaptrack racing, as he called it, in the mining villages of Fife. He said in his younger days he was a "whippet slipper." Me, I had to ask what that was.

"In those days," he said, "we didny start the dogs from traps. They was held by the slipper. One hand on the dog's chest, the other holdin' him by the tail, pullin' his hind parts off the ground. When the gun sounded, the slipper wid toss the dog ta gie it momentum. But on'y if the odds was right and ya wanted him ta win. If ya didny, the slipper might squeeze the poor bastard's balls or gie him a wee jerk on the tail."

Like I said, I had to ask. A few minutes later I excused myself, shaking hands with everybody. Even Maximov. I told Jocky I would see him around the pub and would look out for the others the next time I came to the track.

It was only a quarter past eight. I still had two hours to kill before meeting Pete Swallow at the Traverse. Instead of leaving Powderhall, I went from the enclosed grandstand down to the open area around the track. Just to take a walk and get some fresh air before leaving. The north side of the track has a canopy roof that overhangs cement risers. It's where the local bookies are set up with their chalkboards.

There must have been ten of them lined up a few yards apart. Each had a board with their name on it and areas marked off for trap numbers and odds. I could never figure out just exactly how the system worked. There would be ten to twenty punters crowded around each one of them looking at the board. The odds would change frequently. They would hand money to the bookmaker or his assistant when they wanted to place a bet. I guess it worked on the same principle as the electronic tote board at the far end of the track, but I don't really know.

I strolled along, stopping briefly in front of each bookmaker's board, still trying to make sense out of it. I was standing in front of a board run by "Macbet Ltd" when I heard my name called out loud. It was Rudy.

"Rocco!" he said, shaking my hand. "I didn't know you still came to the track. Still betting number six straight across?" He laughed. I pulled a face.

"I'm here on business," I said.

"Business? You buying a hound?"

"No. I met old Jocky over in the grandstand. He had a Russian with him."

"A Russian? That old git. Where'd he get a Russian?"

"His daddy and Jocky fought together in Spain."

"Did you ask him if they fought the fascists or the anarchist workers in Catalonia?"

"I wanted to, but the geezer is KGB and you know how they are."

"You're joking!"

"Rudy. Would I joke about something like that?"

"I don't know. What are you doing going around meeting KGB agents at dog tracks?" We both laughed. It did sound ridiculous.

"The Perez thing," I said.

"You still mixed up with that?"

"'fraid so. I wanted to get the Soviet version of the story. You know the Montevideo woman claims the KGB killed her husband and kidnapped her."

"I read about it in the *News*. Any truth to it?"

"Probably very little."

"Where does that leave you, then, eh?"

"Downtown Nowhere."

"You know, Rocco, it's funny bumping into you like this. I was going to call you."

"I've been pretty hard to reach, lately."

"Something I heard from one of the ex-thugs I used to hang out with. It's probably nothing. You know how reliable the grapevine is."

"I'd welcome anything at this point, Rudy. What have you got for me?"

Excited shouting broke out all around us. The fifth race had just begun. For the next twenty-nine seconds conversation was impossible. Both Rudy and I turned to the track.

The six bone-lean animals sprinted in confused formation around the track in pursuit of the whirring mechanical bunny. Shouts of encouragement attended each extended stride. I opened my racing programme and quickly glanced at the fifth race. The number six dog was called Red Jet. "Come on, Red Jet," I shouted, pounding my fist in air. He finished fourth.

A moment later relative quiet was restored. I again asked Rudy what he had heard.

"Well, like I say, it's very unreliable. I wouldn't trust it as far as I could throw it."

"Yeah, yeah, okay."

"This bloke called Billy. We used to be wide boys in the old days."

"Forget the old days. Talk about now."

"Aye. I ran into him the day before yesterday. At the pub. After work. I hadn't seen him in years. I almost didn't recognize him. He must've put on two stone."

"Rudy! You're torturing me. Get to the point."

"Okay. But like I said, it's probably just rubbish that

amounts to fuck all. I don't even know why I brought it up."

"Let me be the judge of that."

"Sure. Well, Billy told me that some of his former pals, mine too, I guess. I knew them, but not as well as he did. Billy ran in a different gang before he joined the Mentals."

I grabbed Rudy by the lapels of his jacket. Not hard. Just to get a grip. I shook him. Not hard. Just to let him know. "Rudy! I'm desperate. This case is making me demented. I'm pleading with you. Don't make it any worse. Come to the point, for God's sake!"

"Sorry, Rocco. I just didn't want to build it up into something it's not. You know, raise false hopes."

"Rudy!"

"Right. A couple of Billy's old pals were up on Calton Hill the night Perez got topped."

"And."

"They told him it was a real circus up there. More so than usual."

"How's that?"

"People, guns, fists, bloody heads, screaming. A real first-class fracas."

Rudy paused and looked out on to the the track. The dogs were parading by on their way to the sixth race. Rudy pointed. "Lunar Lad," he said. "Number three. Put your money on that one, Rocco."

"Rudy! Don't leave me hanging. Finish the story."

"That's it finished."

"That's it?"

"Aye. Except that Billy's pals told him they didn't think the folk were Scottish."

"How did they know that?"

"Some of them weren't talking English. They said it sounded like Russian."

"Were they sure? Could it have been Spanish?"

148

"I guess so. You know how these local hoodlums are. They have a hard time understanding English. The only reason I'm telling you is that there was a much bigger row up there than the papers would let you believe. Maybe it's something. Maybe it isn't. I thought you'd like to know."

I stared past Rudy to the track. The dogs were nearing the starting traps. The night was turning chilly. I could feel it. Chilly and blue. Made chillier and bluer by the string of coloured light bulbs that hung around the track. Made me think of winter and Christmas. December. Christmas. Only Santa didn't leave anything under the tree for me.

I bid Rudy a short goodbye. We made a tentative date to show up at Gina and Tony's for a meal in the next couple of days. I told him to get back to me.

I heard the cheering and desperate cries of encouragement as the sixth race was run. I didn't even bother to turn around. I just kept walking slowly toward the exit. I stopped to light a smoke before leaving. Instinctively I turned to look at the tote board. Six came home the winner. Paid 13 to 1. The number four dog placed. The 6-4 forecast paid £6.40 on a 10p bet. I had a feeling it was going to be one of those nights.

CHAPTER TWENTY-SIX

I walked up the darkened streets through Canonmills. I felt like I was being followed, but it was too dark to tell. The shadows could, and probably did, conceal potential mayhem and misadventure. It was the kind of area and night that makes even the most stout-hearted a little paranoid. A sinister fog was beginning to gather around me. My sole friend was the sweet, aromatic fragrance coming from the breweries. It guided me along the streets, giving me a degree of confidence, if not quite courage. It was times like these that revealed to me why Scotland is a land steeped with legends, ghosts and wee beasties that go bump in the night

I hiked up Broughton Street towards more familiar surroundings. I knew that each step was bringing me closer to more people, more life, more safety.

I ducked down the alley to the Trade Unions Club for a quick drink and some friendly faces. The bar was unusually packed. I had forgotten that the function room upstairs was being used as a Fringe venue. A group called Utility Theatre had just finished their performance of *The Sun On Our Backs* and the audience had let out into the pub.

I picked up one of the programmes and read it while I drank a lager-shandy and munched on salted peanuts. The theatre group was from Leicester and their play told the story of "The Dirty Thirty", those thirty miners and their families who remained loyal to the NUM and the strike while their colleagues joined with the Notts miners and worked throughout the dispute. I added it to my growing list of things to see.

I spotted a couple of Annie's SWP comrades drinking at a table near the door. I knew one of them by name. I stopped by to say hello. The one I knew, a young lad who worked around the corner at the Unemployed Council's print shop, invited me to sit with them, but I declined. I told him I was on my way to the Traverse. If I could have figured out how to do it without looking like a jerk, I would've tried to get the lot of them to escort me there.

I said goodbye and returned my glass to the bar before leaving. The smoke, the muffled roar of a dozen different conversations and the snooker on the telly was a scene I had studiously avoided for the most part during my time in Edinburgh. Suddenly, though, it looked strangely appealing to me. I was tempted to drop the whole thing and go back to my self-aspiring humdrum life. A night in the pub would've been a perfect place to start.

I walked out into the night. The fog was thicker. Steamier. If I hadn't known better, I could've been in San Francisco. I walked up Leith Street, around the St. James' Centre, to Princes Street. On a normal night in Edinburgh, the streets would be near-deserted at that hour. And except for the Italian fish and chip shops, the Pakistani groceries and the Chinese take-aways, dark as well. But not in August. I had passed more than a dozen venues by the time I reached Chambers Street. The streets were alive with revellers to-ing and fro-ing between the evening's Fringe offerings. Another hour would see the theatre crowd clock out and the cabaret shift take over. Sometimes they were the same people, although the cabaret crowd did seem to be younger.

I swung down Chambers Street, past the Royal Scottish Museum and came out on George IV Bridge at the top of Candlemaker Row. I looked at my watch. It was ten minutes to ten. Still too early to meet Swallow. I nipped into Greyfriars Bobby, the boozer at the top of Candlemaker Row.

Bobby's, like all pubs in central Edinburgh during the Festival, was crowded. Eventually, I got a half pint of heavy and took a seat near the door to the loo. It was the only place to park. Sitting around a small drinks table near me were some performers from the Fringe. I couldn't help but hear some of their conversation. A couple of them were from a group called Skint Video and the rest were from a nearby venue. The one that was staging the American play about the '60s. I remember ticking it off, because a leaflet I was handed described it as a political rebuttal to the film *The Big Chill*. And if ever a film needed political rebutting, it was that one.

They were all engaged in an animated discussion about their own shows and comparing notes on those they had seen around town. One of them, a tall, good-looking geezer in blue jeans and a white dress shirt was trying to organize a contingent to attend some late-night cabaret at the Pleasance. One of the others, a short woman with cropped hair and a disarming smile, was going over the day's performance of the play she was in.

"The audience was really weird today," I heard her say. "I never got a laugh from that line before."

The man sitting next to her, who looked like a younger version of Jackie Gleason, wagged his finger at her and said, "That's because instead of saying 'our memories sometimes get jumbled', you said 'our memories sometimes get mumbled'. They both laughed. I giggled, too. They stopped and looked at me like I had just stepped off the shuttle from Betelgeuse. I cleared my throat and looked the other way. I drank up and headed for the door. It was 10.10. Before going to the Traverse, I popped into Lillig's, the German cafe just up the street. I had a cup of coffee and a *pfeffernüsse* biscuit to help settle me. The cozy tables, old-fashioned lamps and the big-band jazz coming over the stereo helped a lot. I smoked a cigarette and looked out the window until it was time to leave.

The Traverse, located at the bottom of Bow Street, just off the Grassmarket, has the reputation as the quality Fringe venue for new plays. And it has been an important fixture on the Scottish theatrical scene for twenty years or more.

I walked up the stairs and through the lobby to the cafe. A play was in progress so the joint was pretty deserted. Deserted enough so that I could tell at a glance that Pete Swallow wasn't there.

I got a cup of tea and took a table near the door. I was on my second cigarette when Swallow walked in. I raised my hand and waved, drawing his attention. He came to my table and sat down.

"So glad you decided to come," he said, taking out a smoke from his coat pocket. "Michelle thought you a bit mental this afternoon." He lit his cigarette and blew the smoke toward the floor.

"Where's Lily?" I asked, getting right to the point.

"She couldn't be here, old man. You can understand that. Her life is still in danger. But don't worry, she's safe."

"Well, then she's the only one who is. A lot has happened since you tried to buy me off."

Swallow wrinkled his nose. "Your choice of words. Honestly!"

"Yeah, let's talk about 'honestly', I'd like some straight answers to some very simple questions. No bullshit this time." Swallow's eyebrows began to knit. "Like why did Lily tell me DINA murdered Perez and kidnapped her, but told the press the KGB did it? What was it? A misprint?"

Swallow laughed. "You have a sense of humour. I like that. No, what Lily told the press was the truth. That's why I wanted to see you tonight. Lily and I both thought we owed you an explanation."

"That was downright neighbourly of you."

"Pardon?"

"Skip it. It doesn't translate all that well."

"I see."

"About that explanation. You've cooked up a good one, I hope."

"Conigliaro, you're so cynical. But I guess I shouldn't really blame you. It all must seem like a terrible muddle from your point of view."

"Something like that. That's why I'm here. For you to set me straight. And to see Lily."

"I told you that is impossible."

"Don't take this personally, Swallow, but I'd like a second opinion on whatever it is you're going to tell me."

"My dear fellow. There is only one story to tell. Lily would tell you the same thing if she were able."

"What do you mean 'able'? She been kidnapped again?"

"Good heavens, no. Nothing like that. She's just maintaining a rather low profile until this business is behind us. You can understand that, can't you?"

"Tell me what you've got to say. I'm on a schedule. The Screaming Abdabs are performing at the Fringe Club tonight and I don't want to miss them."

Swallow took a long drag on his cigarette and began telling me the story of how the KGB killed Rodrigo Perez and kidnapped Lily Montevideo. It sounded a lot like the scenario I tried to push up Maximov's nose. It made more sense the way Swallow told it, but still sounded about as credible as a Tory promise to reduce unemployment. He even had an explanation why Lily ended up on a Chilean passenger ship rather than a Russian trawler. He said both the KGB and DINA were on Calton Hill the night of the murder. The KGB killed Perez then split leaving Colonel Vega and his gang to snatch Lily. A real division of labour, that. Swallow must've thought all Americans are stupid.

But there was the Tarkov factor that gave some credence to what he said. And he seemed to have the lowdown on the whole episode. He told it much the same way the district councillor did. But he went further.

"When Rodrigo saw the KGB agents assaulting Tarkov, well, you can imagine how he responded to that."

"He joined in the fight."

"Exactly. It turned into a murderous brawl that left poor Rodrigo with a fatal blow to the head."

"And you think the KGB delivered it?"

"Who else? DINA didn't arrive on the scene until later. No, the only thing on my mind is whether or not the KGB knew who they were murdering at the time."

"What does that mean?"

"It means that it is quite possible poor Tarkov was used from the beginning."

"To lead the KGB to Rodrigo and do in the both of them?"

"It is a possibility. Tarkov had tried to make contact with Rodrigo before, you know. Two years ago in France."

"So you think the KGB planned to get Perez all along."

"I do. I don't think Rodrigo was simply the victim of a brawl in which he was acting the role of a good samaritan."

"Well, what about Tarkov? He officially defected this afternoon."

"I know. He got away from the fracas. Rodrigo didn't. It is as simple as that."

Swallow sounded so sure of himself. So reasonable. I would have to talk to Tarkov to check out his story if I was to challenge him. But with or without the facts I wasn't in any mood to argue with him. It would be like having a fist fight with the fog. What I really wanted from Swallow was the reason why he and Montevideo fed me a phoney story.

"It was a political decision to mislead you,"Swallow said, matter-of-factly. "We knew you were political, but we didn't know where your sympathies lay. We knew it would be difficult even for the anti-tankie left to believe that the Soviet Union would do such a monstrous thing. We didn't want to get into a political argument with you, we wanted to get rid of you. We told you what we thought you would believe."

"Played me for a sap."

"I'm sorry. It was a political expedient. Nothing personal. We were trying to figure out the best way to deal with the situation without making it an anti-communist orgy for the press and government."

"From what I read in the paper, I guess you didn't find it. They creamed both you and the Soviets. In years to come this might become an ideological holiday for the right-wing."

"I regret to admit that you may be right. But it would bother me a whole lot more if the Stalinists hadn't killed Rodrigo. But given that they did, I really can't be bothered about the political fall-out from this. I couldn't control it even if I wanted to. The press are going to write what they want and Thatcher will use it to her advantage regardless of what really happened. That's the way things go."

"Okay, Swallow. That's a real nice story you've told me. Maybe it's even better than the play going on upstairs. But I've been told so many nice stories lately, you'll pardon me if I don't take this one to my building society right away and deposit it."

Swallow looked both hurt and angry. "It's the truth! The bloody, fucking truth!. You've got to believe that!"

"You people must think I have varicose brains. I don't have to believe anyone. Now, tell me where Lily is so I can go hear it from her."

A kind of mild hysteria began to build in Pete Swallow's eyes. He reached across the table and grabbed my arm. "Don't be a fool! Let it alone. You've heard all there is to hear. Leave Lily out of this. For God's sake, man, just bloody forget it and go home!"

"Is this where you pull out some more twenty pound notes and try to buy me off?"

Swallow sighed and his head dropped until his chin almost touched his chest. Then he raised his head and began shaking it slightly from side-to-side.

"You going to tell me where Lily is," I asked. "or just sit there and do aerobics with your neck?"

He looked away from me. "She's in a house in Portobello. I have a car. I'll take you there."

CHAPTER TWENTY-SEVEN

Swallow made a phone call before we left the Traverse. To tell Lily we were coming, he said.

We then drove out to Portobello where Lily was stashed. He didn't want me to know the exact location, so he told Lily to meet us at a small cafe near the beach.

Portobello is twenty minutes from the centre of Edinburgh. Maybe less. It's located along the gentle shores of the Forth at the point where it begins to open up wide. Twenty miles to the east the Forth empties into the North Sea.

Swallow tried to talk me out of seeing Lily the entire way there. He was almost pleading at times. He told me that if I had any decency I would leave her alone and allow her to "begin putting her life back together". But I had some putting back together of my own to do, so I told him to save his breath for someone with more decency.

We pulled to the side of the High Street when we got to Portobello. Swallow took out a pen and wrote something on a little slip of paper. He handed it to me. "You'll find Lily at this cafe," he said. "It's not far from here. Give her about fifteen more minutes."

I looked at him. "Aren't you coming?"

"No!" he said sharply. "You wanted to talk to Lily. Here's your chance."

"I want to talk to both of you. Together."

"Look. Just get out of the car before I change my mind." Swallow reached across me and opened the door.

"Hey! Why so jumpy all of a sudden? You said Lily would tell me the same thing you did. You afraid you might've left something out of your story? Like, maybe the truth."

Swallow lowered his voice and began speaking softly. "Why don't you forget it? Nothing good will come of this. Believe me, nothing. It's over your head. Look. Why don't I run you up to the Fringe Club instead."

"What are you talking about? The Fringe Club."

"The Screaming bloody Abdabs!" he shouted. "Remember?"

"You're nuts," I said, and opened the car door and slid out. Swallow jammed the car into gear and squealed away.

Portobello reminds me of a smaller, quieter version of Atlantic City before the casinos moved in. I don't know the area very well, but I did know the street where the cafe was located. It was near the Fun Park on the beachfront promenade. It would take me only four or five minutes to get there from where Swallow dropped me off so I decided to take the long way around.

I walked east two blocks to the Promenade. It was late, but just about everything was still open. The smell of vinegar and vegetable oil from the fish and chips stands hung in the air at nose level. The electronic ping and blip sounds from the video games at the amusement arcades and bingo numbers crackling from loudspeakers looped around my ears. Teenagers strolling four abreat, smoking cigarettes and eating candy floss, marched lazily up the Promenade. Their parents were drinking at the outdoor lounges and pubs that fronted the Promenade. Lots of activity. A good place to get lost in a crowd.

Despite the lights, it was too dark to see into very

many faces. But you could sense that not too many of them were having the time of their lives. There is something about amusement parks, whether it be the old Playland at the Beach in Frisco or Coney Island in New York or Atlantic City or wherever. Kids walk along the boardwalks consuming junk food, playing pinball, bingo, Tempest — it doesn't matter — lining up for the ferris wheel or the fun house like they are doing shift work and it's only Wednesday. They look more than bored, but less than amused. They look like they are there because it is there and one must do something before going to bed.

I guess amusement parks, seedy and tawdry by definition, are shabby glimpses at what it could've been, might've been in simpler, more prosperous times. Today, they are decaying monuments to those times. Anonymous, rusting physical structures that are roamed and ridden by anonymous individuals just killing time. However, for me, that has always been their appeal. A place where you can go, spend a few bucks and not have your hopes shattered or expectations dashed. Amusement parks are just what they are and everybody knows it. No promises to keep.

I continued along the Promenade stopping briefly to light a cigarette and look at the moonlight. Its yellow rays danced along the crests of the miniature waves of the Forth. I walked a few more yards and the blue light bulbs strung around the perimeter of the Fun Park came into view.

I veered into one of the games arcades that had a fresh air entrance. The big machine full of 2p coins extended almost to the pavement. A continuous sliding motion pushed the coins toward a trough. If you are lucky, they will fall for you when you insert your coin. I reached into my pocket for some change. I popped four of the large coppers into the slot. Nothing fell for me. Next to me

159

a twelve year-old boy was scoring a jackpot of 10p coins on a slot machine.

I came to the entrance of the Fun Park. It was small, mobile and seedy. Sort of like a carny pickpocket, I guess. Just inside the wooden entrance arch was an ear-piercing stall that also sold plastic vampire bats and stickers that said things like "Sex is a misdemeanour. The more I miss it, de meanour I get".

The Elvis Presley disco-ride shattered the night air with an ear-splitting sound that burst through speakers much too small to handle the amplitude. In another life the noise might have been music.

Next to the Elvis ride were the bumper cars, which looked much saner. Directly behind the rides rose two large brick towers. They looked like smaller editions of the cooling towers at the Three Mile Island nuclear power plant. A friend of Annie's from Portobello named Andrew told me they were old, abandoned kilns. They stand outside the Fun Park walls, but I always like to think of them as a carnival ride. "Nuclear Meltdown — the ride of the Eighties".

I was on a ride myself. A roller-coaster to nowhere. I was hoping Lily Montevideo would be able to pull the switch so I could get off.

I walked up the street next to the Fun House toward the cafe. I stopped under a street lamp and took the slip of paper Swallow gave me out of my pocket to double check the address.

A man appeared from somewhere and asked me for a light.

That's happened to me before, in San Francisco and Edinburgh. Everytime it has just been some punter dying for a smoke. Sometimes I oblige them. More often, I just say that I don't smoke and bugger off. I don't like taking chances. But this time was different. The man didn't have a cigarette. He did, however, have a gun.

160

"Come with me," he said, waving his gun toward the door of a house a few yards away.

"I guess you don't want a light then," I said.

"This way." He stuck the gun into my ribs and pushed me with it.

"Okay, okay! You don't have to get physical. This isn't America, you know." I led the way up the steps tp the house. The man opened the door without using a key.

I stepped into a darkened hallway. The man waved his gun pointing down the hall. My feet understood perfectly. The man stopped me in front of a closed door. He knocked and opened it without waiting for a response.

The room was only marginally lighter than the hallway. A soft golden glow spilled from an expensive-looking lamp sitting to one side of a large, dark wood table. I could see the windows were covered with a thick tape. My feet were standing on a piled carpet and I could see the outline of a half-dozen people sitting around the room. I had a feeling none of them was named Lily Montevideo. Before I had a chance to poll the room, one of the persons seated at the table spoke.

"Missed our flight, did we?" It was the Major.

"Yeah," I said. "It was overbooked."

"Pity."

"I could probably make the next one. Ticket's still good."

The Major laughed. "I'm afraid that's not possible, old son."

"Hey, this is Britain. Anything's possible."

"You get on my tits, Conigliaro. And I don't bloody well fancy it."

"Nobody's perfect, Major."

"Look, chalky. We didn't bring you here for beer and sandwiches. Not this time. You've mucked things up. We've got to sort you out. You've got to pay the bill."

161

"Hey! What's with you guys? Didn't you hear? The KGB did it. You guys are clean. Ask Lily Montevideo if you don't believe me. She and Pete Swallow will swear to just about anything. But then, I guess you already know that."

"You're the fly in the ointment. You've got to be dealt with. I was willing to let you fly back to America, but you gave my blokes a right nutting instead. Looks bad down south, if you know what I mean. Even had to call in one of your blokes to help sort you out."

"One of my blokes? I don't have any blokes."

One of the men sitting at the table rose to his feet and walked over to me. "The Major called me in. Wanted to know what he should do with you." The voice was American. I strained my eyes to get a good look at him. He was medium height, white hair, weak chin, thick lips. He looked sort of like William F. Buckley, the conservative *bon viveur*, fly-weight intellectual, yachtsman, novelist and former spook for the CIA. So they say. A taller, older, smarter John Selwyn Gummer, maybe. But like I said, the light was bad.

"I telexed Washington for your file," he continued. "It came back smelling like the Potomac at low tide. Mostly just juvenile stuff from the Vietnam War era. Nothing, really. Just enough for me to hold you in contempt. It was the criminal warrant that made me game for the hunt."

"What criminal warrant? What are you talking about?"

"The Wes-Tex case. I believe you are familiar with it."

The room was chilly when I walked in. The mention of the Wes-Tex case turned it into an igloo. But my face felt hot. Like when you're overdressed and stay in a crowded room too long. Little heat balls pop all over your face. The Wes-Tex case was my swan-song to both the P.I. business and the mother country. That was the case that ended with me on Bryant Street with my witness dying in my arms.

The silence seemed as long as the rainy season in the Hebrides. Finally, I found my vocal chords. "It may have had a messy ending," I said, "but I came away clean. legally, at least."

"Clean?" said the Buckley character. "You skipped the country just about the time the chief defendant went missing. Three months later he turned up dead. Buried near a trail in Marin County. The murder weapon was found two weeks after that. A .38 special. Registered to you. I wouldn't say that was very clean."

The chief defendant in the Wes-Tex case was a man named Lynton Byars, a contract agent for the CIA, who was mixed up with Edwin Wilson a few years ago in that big gun-running operation involving Libya. The firm I was working for nailed him on something different. He was the president of Wes-Tex, a sleazy, fly-by-night outfit that takes poisons from legitimate, up-standing all-American corporations, those that give millions to the arts and starving children, and dumps them in the dead of night somewhere where they think no one will look. I never met Byars and probably wouldn't have recognized him if I caught him in the act. Still, all the memories came back. Again.

The Buckley look-alike was very sure of himself. "So, you see," he said, "you are a fugitive from justice. More than that, really. Byars was a company man. His murder was a special crime. Like killing a cop. And often, the killers of one's own are dealt with in, what shall we call it, an extra-legal fashion. So, you can appreciate my eagerness to help the good Major here when I found out what a catch he had landed."

"Some catch," I said, turning to the major. "If I didn't know you smileys didn't have a sense of humour, I'd say this was a pretty good joke." And indeed, it would have been. But I walked right into it. Like stepping in dog poo with waffle-soled hiking boots. It takes forever to clean them up.

It was becoming clear. I was a perfect fall guy. You didn't have to be a "Mastermind" finalist to realize that I wasn't simply being fitted for a frame, but a "Chicago overcoat" as well.

I had a hard time swallowing that murder-warrant story. Everybody who knew me knew I was in Scotland. Most of them knew my address. If the authorities, any authorities, wanted to find me, they just had to ask. But then there was that spy I read about in the newspaper not long ago who was selling secrets to the Soviets. He used to stay at the Soviet ambassador's residence in Vienna when he was in town conducting business. The CIA knew nothing about it. I don't know, maybe they are that stupid.

But that was secondary. I was to take the fall for Kate Wallace's murder. They were going to throw in Lynton Byars just for good measure. What would the smileys of the world do without the Rocco Conigliaros to tidy up their houses? A chump with dog poo on his shoes. That was me.

I could've tried to talk my way out ot it. I could've said Kate Wallace didn't tell me anything that would connect them with anything. It would've been the truth. I could have said I saw a jogger in a UCLA tee-shirt at the scene of the murder and damn little else. That would also have been the truth. But I knew without asking that the talking stage had long since passed into history.

I could have tried to deal my way out of it, but I didn't have anything to deal with. No hole cards. No letters "to be opened in the event of my death". No nothing. Things had never come to this for Rockford.

The only thing I could think of doing was to make enquiries as to who was responsible for sending me on this one-way journey to meet the "heid bummer". You know, John Knox's boss. It didn't seem to me that the smileys had the collective ingenuity to hatch this all by themselves. And you could forget about DINA.

No, I figured if I was to be the "grout" to patch their falling tiles, I was selected by others. Others with more immediate and personal motives. Someone like Pete Swallow and/or Lily Montevideo. And I think you could just about forget the "/or".

They needed some grout work done, too. It wasn't entirely clear to me just why, but Kate Wallace did and was dropping me hints before a high-velocity bullet terminated our conversation. Without her, I could only make a guess as to what was coming unravelled and why it needed such extreme measures to repair it. Had I the luxury of time I would have gone over to the City Art Centre Cafe and noodled it out over cappuccinos and shortbread. But my life was just about to run out of luxuries like time. And everything else.

The Major tapped a pencil on the table. He spoke without looking at me. "Last chance to buy your way out of this, mate?" he said." What do you say?"

"Sorry, Major. Your price is too high."

"Where's the script?"

"What script?"

"You know bloody well what script. *Ships in the bloody fucking Night*! That's what script!"

"Oh. That script. I wish I knew. I really do."

"The Wallace girl. She know?"

"I don't know. You lot killed her before I could ask. Remember?"

The Major was at the end of his rope. "Leave off, will you? I could turn you over to Vega. He has ways to make blokes like you sing like a bloody budgie. Nasty piece of work, he is. One word from me and he will bring out his instruments."

"If you're trying to scare me, you've succeeded. But no matter what anyone does to me I still don't know where the script is. I don't where any scripts are. The way I heard it only one person knows where it is and we both know she won't talk."

The Major looked at me. "Right," he said. There was the taste of resignation in his voice.

"Besides," I said, "even if I could take you in person to the exact spot where it is located, you wouldn't let me walk away, would you?"

A cynical smile changed the major's expression. "No."

"Well, then. Piss off!"

The Major jumped to his feet and kicked the chair out from under him. But before he could come around the table and throttle me, or do whatever it was that was on his mind, the phone rang. The Major stopped in his tracks while one of the lesser smileys answered it.

He handed it to the major. The Buckley look-alike then started talking to me. I could see his lips pucker and roll, but I didn't hear anything he said. I was listening in on the Major's conversation. It was much more interesting.

"It's out of your hands, now," he said. "That no longer concerns you. We will take care of everything at this end. You just make sure you lot hold up at yours. Time is running out." There was a pause. The Major was growing impatient. "That's our business," he said. "We'll do whatever the situation calls for. No, I am not prepared to tell you what that is. Now, hang up the phone like a good squaddie and remember to keep that gob of yours shut. I don't think I have to review the consequences if you don't." He looked at his watch. "You've got less than eight hours to deliver the goods." The Major then hung up the phone without saying goodbye.

The room fell strangely quiet. The Major signalled to a couple of his subordinates. They came over to the table and he whispered something into their ears. Then one of them left the room.

Next, the Major told the Buckley look-alike to leave, which he did almost before the words left his mouth. Then there was silence again.

The Major leaned back in his chair and lit up a cigarette. He had a triumphant grin on his face. He looked at his watch. "Let's give it another few minutes," he said to the men remaining in the room. Then he pulled his cigarette-packet from his pocket. He laid it on the table and pushed it toward me. "Smoke?" he said.

I took one out of the packet. He tossed a small box of matches at me. They landed within my reach. I took one out and struck it. "Do I get a last request, too?" I said, letting the match burn down almost to my fingertips.

The Major laughed through his nose. "This isn't the bleedin' Foreign Legion, mate."

"Hey! What have you got to lose? It's nothing, really."

The Major smiled. "Why not? I can always say no, can't I?"

"Who was that on the phone?"

"The phone?"

"Yeah. You know. That thing on the table you talk into to."

"A bit dodgy, that one."

"Gi's a break, major. Was it Swallow? Montevideo? Margaret Thatcher?"

The Major laughed outloud. "Margaret Thatcher! That's a bloody good one, that is." A car horn called out from the street. It was soft and short. Little more than a cough, really. The Major looked at his watch. "It's time," he said, to no one in particular.

Two men approached me and grabbed me by either arm and pulled me up from my chair. Another man stood by the door.

The Major rose from his chair. "I'll say my goodbyes

here," he said. Another man who had been sitting silently in the corner all that time joined him as he started for the door. I couldn't get a good look at him, but I knew without asking that it was Colonel Vega. The two of them exited.

Two minutes later, my escort, one on each arm and one leading the way, walked me out of the room, out of the house and into the street. A dark-coloured saloon car was idling at the kerb.

CHAPTER TWENTY-EIGHT

Nobody spoke during the long ride into town. Strange, going back into town, I thought. There were so many remote areas going the other way towards North Berwick. If I was going to bump off a dude, that's where I'd do it. But who was I to tell the experts how to do their job?

Twenty minutes later the car turned up the roadway that leads to the top of Calton Hill. At least these guys had a sense of continuity. Maybe even poetry if I had wanted to think about it.

The saloon car pulled into the car-park beside the Royal Observatory. There were two or three cars scattered around the dark, and otherwise deserted, asphalt.

Before the driver turned off the motor one of the smileys next to me in the back seat taped my mouth shut. When I was led out of the car the same one taped my hands together behind my back. Another one told me to start walking. He pointed to the standing columns of the National Monument. When I didn't move fast enough for him he jabbed me in the back with something hard. I didn't have to ask what it was.

I tried to think of ways to escape. I mean what did I have to lose? I could start running. The worst that could happen was that I would be shot in the back. If I cooperated with them and said "yes sir", a lot — assuming they took the tape from my mouth — I could expect exactly the same thing. A pretty good object-lesson in favour of taking chances in life, I thought. Doing the unexpected and the adventurous. The corollary being, "Go for it, nobody gets out of here alive, anyway". Funny, how life teaches you its little lessons when you can least use them.

Anyway, for some reason, I didn't think about making a break for it. Not seriously, at any rate. Instead, I thought about my life and what I had done with it. It really was flashing in front of me. I thought about San Francisco and growing up. My parents, school, walking along Ocean Beach at sunset, chili-dogs at Playland. I thought about North Beach and Italian fishermen, the fog, Fort Point, *burritos* on Mission Street and the old movies at the Richelieu.

It was all very nice. I probably even had a smile on my face underneath all that tape. A sartorial smile. Then I thought about Annie and my life in Scotland. The cold, the presbyterianism, the lack of movies and the lousy bakeries. And, of course, my present situation on Calton Hill. Then it occurred to me that even though I was staring the big sleep right in the face I'd rather be here in Scotland doing what I was doing than be in San Francisco doing what I did. I mean talk about expatriation. Fear sometimes does strange things to the mind. Maybe that was one of those times. I thought I'd pass out before I reached the monument.

Then I got a second wind that was laced with courage, or foolishness, I'm not sure which. I made up my mind I wasn't going to let these cretins fill me with hot lead like I was some poor lame draught animal. Shit, I felt like I owed my life more than that. I owed it to myself

169

to make these bastards work for their pay.

I stopped just beyond the car-park. One of the smileys poked me in the back again. "Keep walking," he said. "We'll tell you when to stop."

"In your hat, you mother!" I mumbled through the tape. However, it came out, "nnn er at, oo uvver".

The smileys chuckled and one of them shoved me with his hand. I stumbled slightly. When I regained my balance I said to myself, "This is it! I'm going to make a break for it!". I sucked in all the air I could hold. I was just at the point when the inhale was supposed to turn into an explosive exhale and I would make a dash for it when I heard a voice behind me.

"You said you weren't going to hurt him." It was a male voice that sounded like Pete Swallow's, but my head was pounding too loudly to be sure.

I turned in the direction of the voice. So did the smileys. All three of them, went into a crouch and pointed their guns. I couldn't see anyone.

"Who the bloody hell is that?" one of them said.

From a different direction a second voice boomed, tearing the face off the night. "Over here, you assholes!" It was Michelle!

The smileys turned again. That's when the fireworks started. Literally. Two lighted sparkling flares came whooshing through the air from the general direction of the first voice. They landed near our little party and began fizzing, hissing and sparkling. One of the smileys fired into the dark. I think it was just a gesture. Then two more flares came from the same direction. Then two from Michelle's direction. The place looked like the Fourth of July.

I dropped to the ground and started rolling away from the smileys. I didn't get very far when I felt the presence of a body hurtling past me.

"Eat shit, fascist scum!" it said as it whizzed by me.

The next thing I heard was leather hitting flesh, mixed with karate yells and groans from surprised men.

Two of the smileys were down. The third had slugged Michelle in the neck. She was bent over in agony. The standing up smiley moved in to finish her off. I got to my feet and with my hands still tied behind my back rushed him from the blind side ramming him in the small of his back with my head. He made a sound like the Goodyear Blimp being deflated. He took a few wobbly steps before tripping over one of his fallen mates. I followed him and gave him a penalty kick to the head.

I might have added another one for good luck, but a car came to a squealing stop a few yards away. A voice called out, "Get in!" It was Pete Swallow.

"Where's Michelle?" I yelled. The tape had become loosened, but it still came out "airs ichelle?".

"I'm okay," said Michelle coming into view. She looked at the pile of smileys. "We done pretty good, eh?" she said.

"Get into the car!" Swallow repeated. "The both of you. You can gloat over this later."

Michelle followed me into the back seat of the car. She took a knife out of her pocket and cut the tape binding my hands. I then removed the tape from my mouth.

The car had already left Calton Hill and was heading south. Michelle and I looked at each other. She smiled first. I grabbed her hand and squeezed. She squeezed back.

"Thanks," I said. "You saved my life."

"Fuck you!" she said. "I'd've done it for anybody."

CHAPTER TWENTY-NINE

There were cups of hot tea waiting for us when we arrived at a house in Stockbridge. The server was Lily

171

Montevideo. I just sat there in a chair cradling the mug with both hands, holding it almost to my lips. The hot, wet, scented aroma of Earl Grey comforted me. Relaxed me. Perhaps this was the secret behind the British calm and reserve that everybody talks about.

It was a good ten minutes before anyone spoke. Lily Montevideo cleared her throat like she was getting ready to deliver a speech.

"I am sure this must all be very confusing for you," she said. I had been able to piece some of it together and had my suspicions and hunches about other things, but her words struck me as a giant understatement. But I didn't say anything.

"We thought we could control the situation," she continued. "We were foolish to think that. Very foolish."

"And just what was it you thought you could control," I said, regaining my power of speech."

"We thought we could negotiate with the enemy."

"The spooks from DINA and MI6."

"Yes. We thought, I thought, we could make a deal with them."

"Yeah, that was foolish, alright. It almost got me killed."

"I deeply regret what has happened to you, my friend. We have not been very candid with you. I believe Peter provided you with an explanation why I told you DINA killed Rodrigo and then told the press it was the KGB."

"Yeah, he told me, but I didn't believe him."

"You were right not to believe him. But I hope you can find it in your heart to forgive him. Forgive me."

"I don't know. There's not much room in there anymore."

"Peter was trying to protect me. Protect all of us."

"I guess that doesn't include me. He delivered me to the killers in Portobello."

"I tried to talk you out of this business," said Swallow. "Lord knows I tried. You forced my hand."

Lily Montevideo continued speaking. "I am deeply sorry that events went as far as they did. When Peter realized that the enemy had deceived us, that's when he and Michelle went to your assistance."

"I did say thank you." I turned to Michelle.

"I know you have a perfect right to feel bitter and betrayed. But I would hope that you could accept our sincerest apologies for the peril you have been put through."

Swallow took out a cigarette from his coat and lit it. He passed the pack to me. I declined. For the next few moments we all sat around waiting for me to accept Lily Montevideo's apology.

"Michelle killed Rodrigo, didn't she?" I said, breaking the silence. Shattering it. The three of them gasped silently, but I could see it in their faces.

"I beg your pardon," Lily Montevideo said calmly.

"That is way out of line!" added Pete Swallow. "Look. we did apologize. You should accept it and not go around making wild accusations."

"Me making wild accusations! That's a laugh. Everyone in this room but me has been making wild accusations and expecting me to buy them. Look, we know the KGB didn't kill Rodrigo. It's not their style. DINA and MI6 may have wanted to, but a couple things tell me they didn't. You, for one, Ms Montevideo. When a geezer at the dog track convinced me the KGB didn't murder your husband, I asked myself why did you feed the press that story? The answer was quite simply, really. You had to be protecting someone. That's why I haven't got a straight answer since I met the lot of you. The answer to the question who was being protected was just deduction and guesswork. It could have only been Swallow or Michelle. Michelle had the physical tools and disliked Perez. Swallow didn't. That narrowed it down to one." I looked at Michelle. "How about it, Michelle, did you top Rodrigo?"

For the first time since I met her, Michelle was at a loss for words. Swallow tried to cover for her.

"You don't have to say anything, Michelle." he said. He chewed his words angrily. He crushed out his cigarette in a glass ashtray.

Michelle stood up and looked hard at Swallow. "Shut up, Pete!" she said.

"Michelle!" said Lily in a tone that scolded.

"No, Lily. I can't continue to be a part of this anymore." Michelle began pacing up and down the room. "Because of me, Kate was murdered. And tonight Conigliaro nearly bought the farm. We can't go on keeping up this phoney front. We owe this man the truth. The real truth. We owe it to ourselves, too."

"Please, Michelle!" said Lily. "We must protect Rodrigo's memory." She was pleading with her eyes as well as her voice.

Michelle shook her head. Her face seemed to soften. "I know you loved him, Lily," she said. "And I know you had your reasons for doing so, but we've got to face it. He was a shit."

"Michelle!" shouted Swallow. She ignored him.

"As long as he didn't hurt too many people, maybe you could overlook it. But he went too far, Lily. You know it and I know it. I'm really sorry for you, but it's true, damn it."

Lily Montevideo wiped the corners of her eyes with the fleshy part of her palms. Through her tears her eyes begged Michelle to stop, but she knew it had to come out. It helped make it easier on both of them.

"It has to do with Kate Wallace doesn't it?" I asked.

Michelle nodded. "Kate was just the last in a long line of Rodrigo's women." She looked over at Lily.

"Lily, I'm not saying anything I haven't said to you before."

I looked at Pete Swallow. "The row Kate had with Rodrigo didn't have anything to do with the script, did it?" He looked away.

"No!" Michelle said. "They fought because Kate was trying to get away from him. Out of his clutches. And that was something you just didn't do if you were a woman and the great Rodrigo Perez desired you. You didn't have a choice in the matter. He used his authority, his power, his reputation to bulldoze the women in the company and at the school into sexual submission. It was sexual harassment at its worst. Rape in some cases. Remember Susan?"

"Michelle!" shouted Swallow again while nervously fingering a cigarette. "Stop it! What you are saying is irresponsible. If this ever got out, Rodrigo's reputation would be ruined."

"But it's the fucking truth, Pete! What about the reputations of the women he used? What about them? What about Kate?"

Swallow looked away. He muttered something to himself. Michelle walked over to Lily and put her hand on her shoulder. Lily looked up and smiled sweetly. Michelle squeezed Lily's shoulder and then sat down in the chair next to her.

Lily Montevideo sniffed before speaking. "Michelle is a person of great integrity and compassion," she said to me. "I know it pains her very much to say these things, which she knows hurt me very deeply. And in saying them she has placed herself at great personal risk. You see, senor Conigliaro, my husband was an enormously talented man. A genious. But he was flawed in some ways. I knew about his indiscretions for years and I was willing to live with them because of the many good things Rodrigo had to offer me personally and the world of theatre and the audiences that adored him. But this last indiscretion was the proverbial straw that broke the camel's back. His affair with Kate was too public, too insulting for me to bear." She took a paper handkerchief from her pocket and dabbed her teary eyes. Then she took a generous sip of tea and was ready to contine.

During the next fifteen minutes she recreated for me that night on Calton Hill. Some of it I had suspected, some I hadn't. It was Rodrigo and Kate, not Lily, who took that fateful midnight walk. Kate had confided in Michelle earlier that day that she was meeting Rodrigo that evening and was going to tell him that she wouldn't see him any more. She told Michelle she was afraid of what he might do to her.

Michelle, in turn, told Lily about the intended rendezvous and persuaded her that they should follow them and that Lily should confront Rodrigo on the spot.

That all sounded very simple and domestic. I had seen the same situation dozens of times when I was P.I.'ing in Frisco. But something went wrong on Calton Hill. When Kate told Rodrigo she was no longer going to be his playmate he became incensed and started slapping her. The slapping turned into a beating.

That's when Michelle intervened. She rushed him from a few yards away, where she and Lily had been observing them. She pulled Kate away and when Rodrigo then began attacking her that's when she threw a karate chop that landed on his head.

It might have been a fatal blow but there wasn't any time to find out because four men descended on the scene almost immediately. Michelle thought they were the police. They attacked her and the prone Rodrigo, kicking and punching both of them. Michelle lost consciousness for a few minutes. When she came around Rodrigo was lying near her a bloody pulp and both Lily and Kate were gone.

Michelle then went back and told Swallow what had happened. A half-hour later Colonel Vega called. He told Swallow his people had Lily and had witnessed Michelle "kill" Rodrigo. He said he was prepared to make a deal. It was very simple. Lily would be returned and Michelle would be shielded from the police. All Vega wanted in return was the script to *Ships in the Night* and a public statement from Lily that the KGB had killed Perez and kidnapped her.

"My decision to cooperate," said Lily, "had nothing to do with concern for my personal safety. I knew there was nothing Vega could do to me that hadn't been done before. I was prepared for his tortures and would have submitted to them if that had been the issue. But it wasn't. Michelle was the issue. Vega said he would deliver her straight to the police. There was no question in my mind that he wouldn't follow through and do it if we didn't cooperate with him. And I knew the police and the British authorities would have loved to have Michelle as their murderer. I do not know whether she killed Rodrigo or not. If she did it was a tragic accident. She was trying to save Kate and herself from a brutal beating. I saw it with my own eyes. She did what she had to do. But the police would surely not have looked at it that way. Michelle would not be given a fair chance to acquit herself. Politically zealous prosecutors would have prosecuted her to the maximum possible extent."

"So you dealt with DINA. Michelle for the KGB."

"Don't be superior with me, senor."

"I'm not. Just trying to simplify it, that's all."

"It came down to a question of loyalty. Did I betray my friend for some questionable political principle? The principle being to never politically attack, at least not in public, the Soviet Union. To me senor, that kind of so-called principle is wrong. Politically and morally. As a

177

person in theatre I oppose censorship in all forms. And my commitment was to my friend, not some political ideal that is little more than empty rhetoric. No, senior, I take my friends and my politics more seriously than that. There was no question about what I should do. I discussed it fully with Peter. He agreed completely." She looked at Swallow for corroboration.

"That's right, Conigliaro," he said. "Michelle's life was at stake. Fitting up the KGB seemed like a rather small price to pay. Especially considering all the bother the Soviets and their various representatives have given us over the years. And they were there on Calton Hill. That part is true."

"But you don't know if they were there to blast Rodrigo."

"I can surmise. I mean, what is the political difference whether Rodrigo was beaten up by Stalinist hooligans in Paris or kicked to death by DINA and MI6 agents in Edinburgh?

Swallow had a point. Sort of like George Orwell when he wrote *Homage to Catalonia*. Who was ultimately responsible for the defeat of the Spanish revolution? Franco, or Stalin's agents? A question that still gets up a lot of noses.

I don't know the answer. The Soviets have done a lot of nasty murderous things in the name of socialism. Remember the purge trials? Czechoslovakia? Hungary? And the Americans and the Brits, to be sure, have done more than their share of criminally barbaric things in the name of democracy. Grenada. Nicaragua. Vietnam. Northern Ireland. South Africa. The list is endless. There is a difference but sometimes it is awful hard to tell. And what does that difference mean? To be devoted socialists as Perez and Montevideo had been for all those years, and to suffer attacks from both sides of the political street, who was I to place a judgement on what

178

Lily did? Even if it did appear to play into the hands of the reactionaries

Lily Montevideo was right. Life in the political trenches is not just a collection of politically correct positions wrapped in some kind of weird and perverted morality. That's what the Stalinists and the Maoists and the Trotksyists and the anarchists have all used, in one way or another, at one time or another, to try and bully their way into the hearts and minds of the working class. In the case of Eastern Europe it's just plain bullying. If you get the people by the balls, their hearts and minds will follow. That was American foreign policy in Vietnam. Chile, too. And that was one subject Lily Montevideo knew a whole lot about.

So, she risked an international incident and wholesale denunciation by the left to save her comrade. Her confidant. Her friend. There was something about that I could like. For generations, too many friendships have washed up on the polluted shores of "political principle". Folk who "betrayed" their principles, who were friends and activists in the Communist Party, or any party, and had the courage to stick by each other even if one of them dissented from the party line on some important question and was forced out of the organization, as they surely were. And are. People who wouldn't let Marxist-Leninist heavy breathing, ruthless expulsion, verbal damnation and moral guilt-tripping — all dredged up in the name of some phoney political righteousness — destroy their bonds of friendship.

So, I was glad to see someone like Lily Montevideo standing up for friendship. For personal loyalty at the risk of being tarred with the Marxist-Calvinist brush of political betrayal. Especially when standing up for a friend meant personal humiliation for herself. And perhaps even the death of a god.

Rodrigo Perez would now join the ranks of mortal

flesh and blood. It is ironic that it took his death to do so.

I'm all in favour of having heroes, but gods are something different. They're a dangerous lot, especially when they use their godliness to throw their weight around. And Perez threw his around in the worst way.

Rodrigo Perez was no god. He was a brilliant playwright who inspired, educated and entertained a generation. But he was also a brute who pushed around a lot of women. The sooner people knew that, the sooner he would be de-deified. And unless the middle-class, single-issue feminists go off their heads and start organizing censorship/boycott campaigns against his work, it would be a better situation all around. For Lily. For those who worshipped him. For political theatre.

"So," I said, after a long silence, "what happened to the second part of the deal with Vega?"

"You mean the script?" Swallow said.

"Yeah."

"There is no script, senor," said Lily Montevideo.

"What?"

"It was all in Rodrigo's head," she continued. He made up the story about the script to protect himself and the production."

"How'd he do that?"

"Rodrigo had been receiving death threats ever since we went into rehearsals for *Ships in the Night*. Not actual verbal threats, but there were physical signs. He was followed everywhere he went and there were a number of mysterious accidents. Only they weren't accidents. Rodrigo was convinced it was our old enemies from DINA. And once the Home Office started harassing us he believed the British government were also involved. He was sure there would be attempts on his life before the play opened.

"But as long as DINA and the Home Office thought

a script existed, they would try to obtain a copy of it. If, however, they knew none existed, they could, if they chose, just eliminate Rodrigo to ensure the information never reached the public."

I turned to Swallow. "Did you know this?"

He nodded. "It was an insurance policy. To protect Rodrigo and the production, at first. Then, when he was gone, we used it to deal for Lily and Michelle."

I looked over at Michelle. "You've got a couple of real friends here, I'd say."

She looked at me quizzically. Then her face puffed up a bit and her eyes filled. "I know," she said. Her voice cracked and she rotated her jaw. "They went to the wall for me. I knew they would, but it chokes you up just the same." She looked away. "I just feel so damn rotten it had to turn out this way. Rodrigo, and then Kate."

Her voice trailed off. Lily rose from the couch and went to her. She put her arm around Michelle's shoulder and whispered something comforting in her ear. Michelle turned and they embraced. I tried not to stare. It was a private moment in a public place.

"So," I said to Swallow, "I guess that's it, eh?" Swallow didn't say anything. "Do the bad guys know there's no script?"

Swallow shrugged his shoulders. "I don't know. And I don't much care."

"Well, I don't know, either. But if they think there is a script floating around somewhere, they might get sore that you haven't lived up to your part of the bargain."

"What can they do?"

That sounded odd to me. "What can they do?" They killed Perez and Kate Wallace and nearly sent me to the tartan valhalla. I should think they could do quite a lot. But Swallow didn't seem to care. As far as he was concerned it was over.

He said something about catching the early morning

train to London. Lily said something about re-mounting the play after the Festival. I said something about catching some sleep.

I got up and walked to the door. I said goodbye, but no one seemed to take much notice. They were preoccupied with their own problems. I didn't take it personally.

CHAPTER THIRTY

I walked to Raeburn Place to catch a cab. I knew it might be a while, so I had a smoke. Well, that was that, I said to myself. Not as conclusive as catching a husband with his pants down or an embezzler with his hand in the till, but finished just the same. Fin. Finito. The end. Two murders, three kidnappings (two of them mine), brushes with intelligence agents from four countries and lies too numerous to count.

But it was over. Personal loyalty scored a technical knock-out over political rhetoric. That was good, wasn't it? Even if the smileys from DINA and MI6 appeared to have scored more goals. They were sitting pretty even if I did get away from them and they didn't get a copy of Perez's script.

Michelle turned out to be a good egg. And Lily Montevideo came clean with me and turned out to be a lady with a lot of integrity. And Pete Swallow. Well, I guess some of the other two had to rub off on him.

I could now go to the Fringe and see Mark Miwurdz or anybody else I wanted with the comforting knowledge that the good guys had stood up to be counted. So, then why did I feel so lousy and unsatisfied?

A taxi finally came and I took it to Annie's. It was late and she was not at all chuffed when I arrived at her door at 2 a.m. But she let me in anyway. Almost instinctively, she put the kettle on, made some toast and put out a plate of my favourite biscuits.

I recapped the last thirty hours of my life for her. I did it almost as much to make sense out of it for myself as to inform her. I tried to find the meaning to things I could still only guess at. Like why DINA and MI6 felt they had to kill Kate Wallace. That was something neither Swallow nor Lily made clear. I mean she wasn't killed because she was dumping Perez. Was it because she was a witness to his murder and couldn't be relied on to abide by the KGB-for-Michelle deal? But that didn't make sense. Why wouldn't she go along with it? She and Michelle were very close. She confided in her about her rendezvous with Perez on Calton Hill. She would have been as loyal as Swallow and Lily.

It must have been that Kate was gunned down because the smileys didn't want her to talk to me. Maybe they feared she would reveal the truth about what happened on the night of the murder and that would blow their deal with Swallow and Montevideo right out of the water. Maybe. But realistically, what could I have done with such information. Who did the smileys think I was? Jim Rockford?

"Maybe it was you they wanted to kill," said Annie, "and not Kate. Did you ever think of that?"

The words pierced the air like crystal chimes tolling for the dead. They reached out and gave me the slap of life, recalling me from some dark and vaguely known place.

I jumped up from my chair and rushed over and kissed Annie on the mouth.

"What's that for?" she said startled.

"For being here when I needed you. For having a sister on Skye. For making me read *Socialist Worker*. For being such a bonnie wee lassie."

Annie shook her head. "Ach. You really are a bampot."

CHAPTER THIRTY-ONE

The early morning train for London leaves Waverley at 7.25. I was there at 7.10. So was Pete Swallow. I watched him get out of a cab and go into the newsagent. He bought a *Guardian* and started for the departure platform. He was travelling light. Just one shoulder bag and a brown package tucked under his arm.

I followed him at a safe distance. He stopped to check the departures board and pulled back his sleeve to look at his watch. A small bagpipe band was standing in formation in the plaza in front of the board. They were decked out in their colours, from their Glengarry caps to their thick black cordovans. They were playing "Scotland the Brave."

Swallow stood nervously waiting for the inbound train to arrive. He was at least fifteen minutes early and was virtually standing alone on the platform. A few minutes passed and a man emerged from the area near the pipeband, I didn't get a good look at him, but I knew who he was. Felt who he was. He was wearing a pair of slacks and a windbreaker. The first time I saw him he was wearing a UCLA tee-shirt. He was approaching Swallow. It was right out of the movies. I walked around the pipe band to get a better look.

The man was only twenty-five paces away from Swallow. When Pete saw him he started walking toward him. He had only taken a few steps when I heard his name called out. It carried above the whine of the pipes and the thump of the drums. Pigeons scattered from the rafters at the sound. Several travellers stopped to look. It was Michelle and she was running toward him.

Swallow froze when he saw her. He turned and looked at the man approaching him. Then he began to run. He ran past the man, through the pipe band and onto the loop-road that leads in and out of the station.

The approaching man began running after him. Michelle was running at Swallow from a different angle. I joined in the chase from a third. The approaching man pulled something from his coat. It looked like a weapon. I don't know if he fired it at the fleeing Swallow. I didn't hear a shot, but that doesn't mean anything. Suddenly, Swallow slowed and began running erratically. But he was still running. Michelle and I closed in on him, as did the jogging smiley.

Swallow still kept running. He weaved onto the platform directly under the pedestrian passageway that connects the Waverley Steps with Market Street and the City Art Centre.

There was a lot of noise. People were screaming, bag-pipes were moaning, locomotives were hissing and cabs were speeding up the loop-road. Above it all was the low, throaty churning of an approaching train.

Swallow staggered to the edge of the platform. Michelle cried out for him to stop. The jogging smiley had stopped thirty feet away. Swallow turned when he heard Michelle call his name. His face was all twisted up. He had a bewildered and frightened look. He opened his mouth as if he were about to say something, but nothing came out. Instead he dropped his shoulder bag and the brown package at his feet, turned and took one more step. He tottered for a moment before disappearing over the edge of the platform. The train passed an instant later. The screech of the brakes and the screams of the people who were close enough to know what happened curdled the air.

I joined Michelle at the platform. The smiley had disappeared.

"Oh, Pete!" she bellowed. "Why? Why? Why?" She fell to her knees and picked up the brown package.

A crowd was forming on the platform. It was only a matter of minutes before the place would be crawling with cops. I took Michelle by the elbow and hustled her up the stairs to the walkway that led to the Waverley Steps.

We didn't stop until we reached Princes Street Gardens. I sat her down on a bench and offered her a smoke. It seemed to calm her some. I lit one for my self. It seemed to calm me some, too.

Michelle stared up at the buildings at the top of the far side of the Gardens. "Why did he do it?" she repeated several times.

I pointed at the package. "That's the script, isn't it?"

She nodded her head. "He had it all the time. He told me he didn't, but I knew."

"Kate?"

"Yeah. She told me. Rodrigo told her he gave it to Pete with instructions to keep it in a safe place and to deny its existence if it became necessary."

"More insurance policy?"

"Yeah, something like that. As long as Rodrigo was alive, and later when the pigs kidnapped Lily, it was to our advantage to admit to its existence. But with Rodrigo dead and Lily free, it became a liability. So, I guess that's when Pete decided it didn't exist."

"And Lily went along with this?"

Michelle shook her head. "She didn't know it existed in the first place. Rodrigo told her he invented it to protect himself and the play. Lily believed him."

"But you didn't."

"At first, I did. But then Kate told me Pete had it."

"Did you tell Lily?"

"I tried, but she wouldn't listen. She trusted Rodrigo too much. I used to hate that about her. But what could I do? Besides, she said it really didn't matter."

"How's that?"

"Because Rodrigo had shown Lily the monologues and she had memorized them."

"Did Swallow know that?"

"I don't think so. He wanted to think he was the only one with the script. I guess it was his ego."

"Why didn't you bring it out last night when Lily told me the script never existed?"

"I didn't want to hurt her any more. I just let Pete have his way."

"But you didn't trust him, either. That's why we both showed up at the train station this morning, right?"

"I knew he had the script. I knew he had cooked up the deal with the pigs. And I knew he was in a big hurry to get back to London."

"You smelled a rat. Just like me."

"I don't know. Pete was a strange guy. Most people didn't like him, you know. He was one of those public school snobs who became political. He brought a lot of his pissy, upper-class ways with him. But he was a decent guy. I trusted him as much as I trusted any man. I believe he really wanted to protect Lily and me and the company when he was dealing with the pigs from DINA and MI6. Shit, Pete could be a first-class jerk at times, but he was a square-shooter."

"Why do you think he wanted to catch the early train?"

"That's what I came to find out."

"Did you get a good look at the guy who was chasing Pete?"

"No."

"I did. It was the same hitter who gunned down Kate."

187

"The bloody bastard!"

"Who? Swallow or the smiley?"

Michelle didn't answer. Her jaws locked together and tears began spilling from the corners of her eyes.

"We've got to face it, Michelle. Pete may have meant to meet that man and give him the script."

"Don't you think I fucking know that?" she said angrily through her tears. She sniffed and wiped her eyes.

"But then again, maybe he was just trying to get out of town before the smileys pulled his plug and he just didn't make it."

"Don't hand me that shit, man. Okay?"

"Look. It could've happened that way. It doesn't sound likely, I agree, but who's to say?"

"You know, Conigliaro, you're still a big pain in the ass."

I've been called worse. And by her. But I did have a point. Who was to say? The obvious was that Pete Swallow was going to meet Kate Wallace's assassin to give him the script. What for? For money? To save his own skin? Or maybe to keep his part of the bargain with DINA and MI6 to keep Michelle from the nick. We'll never know.

What I did know was that Swallow, in making the deal, went over the top. He got sucked in, manipulated, maybe even "turned", as they like to say in the spy business. It was Swallow that alerted the smileys to me and when I started doing some serious nosing around he must have gotten frightened that I might tumble to his game and so asked them to get me out of the way. Maybe he just wanted me scared off, but there was that jogger at the beach who was sent there to do a lot more than scare me.

It was almost a sure thing that it was Swallow who called the Major at the house in Portobello. He was trying to back away from it. Maybe he felt things had

188

gone too far and didn't want another death on his hands. I can only speculate.

It was ironic in a way. Swallow trying to deliver the script to the smileys. Like Lily said, it didn't really matter. Even if the bad guys got their hands on the political dynamite in the Perez monologues and took steps to "grout" the political damage they threatened to cause, Lily Montevideo had them committed to memory. And the Major, Colonel Vega and I knew that nothing short of death would stop her from mounting a production of the play at some future date. The play would go on. Sometime. Somewhere. And if I knew either Lily Montevideo or Michelle, it would be sooner rather than later.

Michelle stood up. She went to a rubbish bin located at the end of the bench and took out a discarded newspaper. She shredded it and placed it in a neat little pile on the path. Then she reached into her pocket and took out a box of matches and set fire to the pile. Next, she tore open the package and began crumpling up the pages and dropping them onto the fire.

"Look, you bastards!" she yelled. "I'm burning the fucking thing! It's over!. You lost!"

I looked around while Michelle continued her loud ritual tossing a few pages at a time onto the fire. I saw two men at the top of the walk near the flower-clock entrance to the Gardens. They had binoculars. I could guess who they were.

"You lost! You bloody assholes!" Michelle dropped the last pages onto the fire. We watched them burn in silence. The wind swirled and took large bits of blackened ash upward. They floated lazily in the direction of the two men with the binoculars.

When it was all done, Michelle extended her hand. "Rocco!" she said sternly. "I'm sorry I called you a greaseball."

189

I took her hand. "Michelle!" I said mocking her stern-
ness. "I'm sorry I threw my rubber nose in your lap."
We shook hands. Then, as if on some pre-arranged signal, we threw our arms around each other and embraced.
It lasted less than an instant.

Michelle kicked the ashes at her feet. She looked
at me, did something with her lips that reminded me
of a smile and then turned and walked briskly away. I
wanted to call out for her to stop. There was so much
more I wanted to talk to her about. But my vocal
chords went on strike. A small lump worked its way up
my oesophagus and lodged in the back of my throat.
I watched her walk away towards the Mound until she
disappeared into the distance.